D1328174

# Spotting
# TREES

# Spotting
# TREES

## IN BRITAIN AND EUROPE

*An illustrated guide to the top 100 trees*

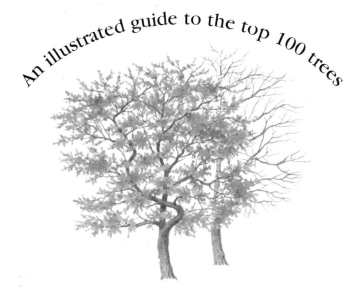

CONSULTANT: TONY RUSSELL

LORENZ BOOKS

This edition is published by Lorenz Books

Lorenz Books is an imprint of
Anness Publishing Ltd
Hermes House
88–89 Blackfriars Road
London SE1 8HA
tel. 020 7401 2077; fax 020 7633 9499
www.lorenzbooks.com; info@anness.com

© Anness Publishing Ltd 2005

UK agent: The Manning Partnership Ltd
6 The Old Dairy, Melcombe Road
Bath BA2 3LR
tel. 01225 478444; fax 01225 478440
sales@manning-partnership.co.uk

UK distributor: Grantham Book Services Ltd
Isaac Newton Way
Alma Park Industrial Estate
Grantham
Lincs NG31 9SD
tel. 01476 541080; fax 01476 541061
orders@gbs.tbs-ltd.co.uk

North American agent/distributor: National Book Network
4501 Forbes Boulevard
Suite 200, Lanham, MD 20706
tel. 301 459 3366; fax 301 429 5746
www.nbnbooks.com

Australian agent/distributor: Pan Macmillan Australia
Level 18, St Martins Tower
31 Market St, Sydney, NSW 2000
tel. 1300 135 113; fax 1300 135 103
customer.service@macmillan.com.au

New Zealand agent/distributor: David Bateman Ltd
30 Tarndale Grove, Off Bush Road
Albany, Auckland
tel. (09) 415 7664; fax (09) 415 8892

Publisher: Joanna Lorenz
Editorial Director: Helen Sudell
Project Editor: Simona Hill
Copy Editor/Additional Text: Alison Bolus
Editorial Reader: Shirley Kerr
Illustrators: Peter Barrett, Penny Brown, Stuart Carter, Stuart Lafford, David More,
Anthony Duke (location maps)
Design: Howells Design Ltd
Production Controller: Wanda Burrows

1 3 5 7 9 10 8 6 4 2

# CONTENTS

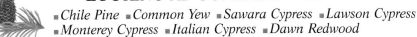
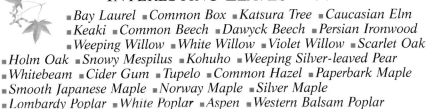

# Introduction

Whether you live in a village, town or city, by the sea, in the countryside or in the mountains, there will be plenty of different trees around you that you can learn to identify.

▲ You can collect seeds, or nuts, from the countryside in autumn. Find a tree that you like the look of and look below its crown for fallen nuts. This tiny oak tree began life as a nut known as an acorn.

◀ The oak tree is one of the world's best-known trees and a very familiar sight in Europe. It can live for hundreds of years.

Spotting trees is an activity you can share with all your family. When you are out together, keep a look-out for different shaped trees, and notice their overall shape, the size of their leaves, the colour and texture of their bark and whether they have any flowers, fruit or cones. All these aspects will help you to work out which trees they are. Take a notebook and pencil with you when you go, and look out for the following characteristics, all of which will help you to identify the species of tree you are looking at. First look at the profile of the tree, is it tall and column-like, or does it have a spreading crown? Does the tree have needles or leaves? What shape and size are they? Are the leaves smooth, rough or hairy? If it's winter, does the tree have any leaves or are the branches bare? At what point on the trunk do the branches appear? Is the bark smooth, rough, cracked or papery? Does the tree have nuts, berries, larger fruits, cones or flowers? What shape, size and colour are they?

## Identifying trees

With your notes of the trees that you have seen in front of you, compare them to the trees in this encyclopedia. All the facts you need to know about the shape, trunk, bark, buds, leaves, flowers and fruit of each tree are included so that you will have no difficulty identifying your "find".

Many trees have interesting features that distinguish them from other trees and make them easier to identify. For example, the handkerchief tree has a large white bract that hangs from the branches to look like a handkerchief hanging from a sleeve. The bract can be seen all over the tree in spring and because this tree grows very tall, it looks impressive.

▼ *Trees grow very tall compared to humans, but often their parts, such as flowers, twigs, stems and leaves, are small and grow near enough to the ground for us to be able to identify them.*

▲ *If you take a drawing book and some colouring crayons with you when you go out for a walk, why not make a rubbing of some leaves? A rubbing will show the ridges, veins and shape of the leaf and help you identify the tree. To make a rubbing, place the flattened leaf upside down between two pieces of paper. Put the paper and leaf sandwich on a smooth surface. Rub the crayon over the surface and the markings will be revealed.*

## How this book works

The 100 trees chosen for this book have been grouped into chapters according to their most interesting features. Many conifers tend to grow together, so we have grouped them into one chapter so that you can compare them easily. Other trees have distinctive leaves and attractive flowers, or fruit. Some trees are amazing, they live for hundreds of years, or grow very tall, and we have included these in a separate chapter. Each tree is illustrated with a map, so that you can see where in the world it originated, even though it may now grow thousands of miles away from its homeland. There are also full details about how a tree lives, grows and dies, as well as information about the role each part of the tree has in its survival.

# All About Trees

Trees grow all over the world, in geographical areas as different as mountains and deserts, and in many climates from the coldest northernmost lands to the hottest tropical rainforests. There are thousands of different species of trees in the world and each species has learnt to adapt to the environment in which it lives. The overall appearance of a tree, its height and growth rate, the shape and size of its leaves and flowers, the texture of its bark, even the roots it grows have all been determined by factors like its altitude, the local weather conditions and the animals that might feed on it.

# What is a Tree?

*All trees have three things in common, no matter how different their appearance, or the size that they grow to: they all have a single woody stem known as a trunk, and they all have roots and leaves.*

All trees grow from a seed, which can be a nut, or can be found inside a fruit produced by the tree. The fruit can be small, such as a tiny berry, or it can be large, like an apple. To begin life a seed needs the right conditions to sprout, or germinate. There must be nutrients, water and light. Many seeds can live in the earth for years before they begin to germinate. Once they do, they grow roots that move downwards and a stem that grows upwards towards the light. The stem or trunk develops branches which eventually divide to become smaller. At the ends of the branches, twigs grow. Along the sides of the twig and at the end of it, buds develop in spring. These become flowers or leaves. The flowers attract pollinating birds and insects to the tree with their strong scent or bright colours. Once pollinated the flowers drop from the tree and in their place grow fruits, containing the seeds that will begin the cycle again.

▲ *A deciduous tree, such as this apple tree, is one that loses its leaves in winter. The winter profile of the tree is shown behind the summer profile, which shows how the tree looks when all its leaves are fully formed in the height of the season.*

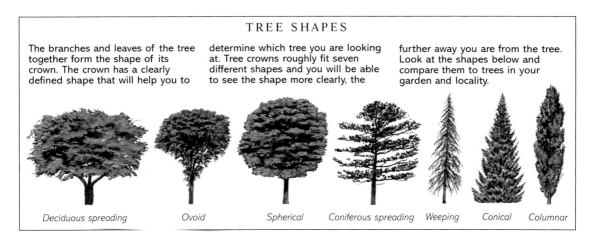

## TREE SHAPES

The branches and leaves of the tree together form the shape of its crown. The crown has a clearly defined shape that will help you to determine which tree you are looking at. Tree crowns roughly fit seven different shapes and you will be able to see the shape more clearly, the further away you are from the tree. Look at the shapes below and compare them to trees in your garden and locality.

*Deciduous spreading*   *Ovoid*   *Spherical*   *Coniferous spreading*   *Weeping*   *Conical*   *Columnar*

## Parts of a tree

Each tree, no matter what its shape, is made up of a trunk covered in bark and a crown covered in branches, twigs and leaves. To keep them upright trees have roots that spread into the ground.

*Leaf*

*Needles*

*Fruit and leaves on a twig.*

*Leaves and needles grow on twigs, and twigs grow on branches.*

*Bud*

*Buds will open into leaves or flowers.*

*Flowers attract birds and insects to the tree.*

*Young leaves*

*Tree trunks are covered in bark, which is like a skin. It can be smooth or rough.*

*Stem*

*These wings contain tiny seeds. The wings help propel the seeds on the wind.*

*Roots*

*Nut*

*Nuts are the seeds of trees. They fall to the ground and may grow to become new trees.*

*The roots grow below ground level and spread outwards and downwards.*

*Berries are one type of fruit.*

9

# Roots

*Tree roots have three main jobs. They stop the tree from falling over. They feed the tree by sucking up water and minerals from the soil, and they also store the starchy food produced by the leaves.*

▲ *Mature trees develop fascinating root systems. These roots are covered in moss above the ground.*

Roots rarely reach more than 3m/10ft down into the ground, no matter how tall the tree is. Instead, they spread sideways just under the surface. This is because it is the top layers of soil that contain the minerals and moisture that trees need to survive.

The first root that every tree grows is called a tap root. Tap roots grow straight down and can extract moisture and minerals from the soil. Within days of the tap root emerging from a seed, side roots (known as laterals) grow off the tap root and begin to move sideways through the top layers of soil.

*Most lateral roots stay close to the surface for the* ▼ *whole of a tree's life. Those that grow directly from the base of the trunk may be over 30cm/1ft across, though by the time they are 1m/3ft away from the trunk they taper to around 10cm/4in across, and at 4m/13ft away they are usually under 5cm/2in across, and far more soft and pliable. Fine roots may spread to anything up to 30m/100ft away.*

*Roots are thickest* ▶ *near the trunk and very fine at their ends. Each root has millions of hairs that take up water.*

### SEE HOW ROOTS GROW

**You will need**
a glass jar, blotting paper, broad (fava) bean, water, a light source

1. Curl a piece of blotting paper to fit inside the jar and fit it to one side. Push the broad bean halfway down the glass.

2. Add water to a depth of 2cm/1in and stand the jar in a light, warm place.

3. When the seed germinates, you can see the root growing downwards. Turn the jar so that the root points to the right. What will happen next?

4. See how the root has changed direction and is growing downwards again.

# Trunk and Bark

*What makes a tree different from all other plants is the tough, woody framework it raises above the ground. As each year passes, this framework gets bigger as the trunk and branches expand upwards and outwards.*

A tree's bark is like a skin. It is a corky waterproof layer that protects the inner cells from disease, animal attack and, in the case of redwoods and eucalyptus, forest fires. It has millions of tiny breathing holes in it called lenticels, which can become clogged up in polluted areas. Until trees stop growing through old age, their trunk and branches constantly get longer and wider. As they grow, so the bark grows too, though older trees tend to have splits and cracks in their bark where the bark has not grown as fast as the tree.

## How the trunk works

Under the bark is a soft spongy layer called phloem, which carries the sap – sugary liquid food – from the leaves to the rest of the tree. Under the phloem is a very thin layer called the cambium, which is where all the tree's growth takes place. Cambium cells are constantly dividing, producing phloem cells on the outside and wood cells, or xylem, on the inside.

The xylem has two parts: the outer sapwood, made of living cells that transport water and minerals from the roots to the leaves, and the inner heartwood, which is composed of dead cells.

Indian horse chestnut

Eucalyptus

Cork oak

▶ ▲ *Bark is often the main identifying feature of a tree in winter. The Indian horse chestnut bark has cracks over its surface and a rough texture. Eucalyptus bark is smooth, but mottled, and the cork oak bark has channels in it. The birch bark on the right is smooth, white and papery.*

Birch

◀ *If you see a felled log when you are out, look for insect holes. Many insects and larvae burrow into wood. These tunnels were made by bark beetles.*

### HOW BIG IS THAT TREE?

1. Take a piece of rope to measure the trunk. Put it around the tree and keep your finger on the place where the rope overlaps.

2. Lay the rope out straight on the ground and measure to the place you have marked. This equals the distance around the trunk (girth).

# Buds

*The buds act as protective sheaths, or cases, for the growing tips of trees during the coldest months of the year. In winter, even though deciduous trees will have shed their leaves, they can still be readily identified by their buds.*

▲ *The first leaves of a sycamore tree break from the bud in early spring.*

▲ *Wing nut bud.*

▲ *Horse chestnut bud.*

▲ *The Indian horse chestnut bud opens to reveal long, thin leaves, which are coated in a soft down.*

The normal pattern for most temperate trees is for a period of growth, usually in spring and summer, followed by a period of rest, during the time of year when the climate is least favourable for growth. Across Europe, this is during the cold and dark of winter.

At this time of year, even though many trees have shed their leaves, it is still possible to identify which tree you are looking at from the shape and colour of the tree's buds. Not all buds look the same, and many are arranged differently on the twigs. For example, some buds may be positioned opposite each other on a twig, others may be arranged in clusters or positioned alternately (diagonally opposite each other).

## Protective sheath

During early autumn, as the growing season approaches its end, the last few leaves to be produced by the tree are turned into much thicker but smaller bud leaves, known as scales. These toughened leaves stay on the tree after all the other leaves have fallen off, and they form a protective sheath around the growing tips of a tree, called the meristem. This sheath is knows as a leaf-bud. Its thick scales are waterproof and

*This cross-section of a leaf ▶ bud shows the tiny leaves all folded over each other inside the protective coating of the bud.*

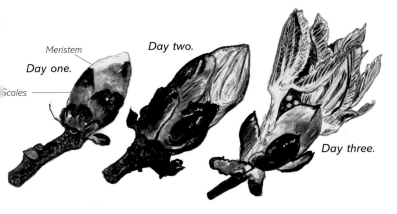

Meristem

Day one.

Day two.

Scales

Day three.

◀ *The sticky buds of a horse chestnut tree will open over a period of three days in springtime.*

growing season, the last leaves to be formed stop growing before they are fully developed. They wrap themselves around the meristem, and are protected from the weather by a thick layer of hair. When spring comes, the protective leaves simply start growing again from where they left off.

Some conifers, such as the western red cedar (*Thuja plicata*) and Lawson cypress (*Chamaecyparis lawsoniana*), have no distinct buds at all; instead they produce little packets of growing cells, which are hidden beneath the surface of each frond of needles.

Trees without buds do not grow as quickly as those that have buds, but they grow for a longer period of time. At the end of the growing season, both trees will have achieved the same amount of growth.

overlap each other. Often a coating of wax, resin or gum over the top of the bud provides another layer of defence against rain and frost. Look at trees in autumn and you will see that the tips of the branches have tiny buds or shoots growing on them.

## Inside the bud

During the cold winds and frosts of winter, the bud protects the growing material for next year: a tiny shoot and some tiny leaves are all carefully and tightly folded over one another, and in some species there are tiny flowers protected inside the bud too.

## The growing season

As spring arrives, the buds open and the leaves begin to emerge. For all trees, the trigger for this to happen is increasing warmth and longer daylight hours. Once the buds are open, some trees tend to have a single growth spurt immediately after the leaves emerge. This can mean that they do all their growing for the whole year within the first four weeks of spring.

## Trees without buds

Not all trees produce buds. Some, such as the wayfaring tree (*Viburnum lantana*), have "naked" buds with no bud scales. At the end of the

▼ *Sweet chestnut buds.*

▼ *Magnolia bud.*

▼ *Violet willow buds.*

# Leaves

*Every tree has many leaves providing a canopy around the branches and casting shade on to the ground. Leaves grow from buds on the branches. They have a short life cycle, even on evergreen trees, where the tree is covered in leaves all year round.*

Each leaf generates food, which the tree uses as energy for living and growing. At the same time the leaves absorb carbon dioxide and emit oxygen.

## The outer leaf

The epidermis, or skin, of a leaf is coated in a waxy covering called the cuticle, which prevents the leaf losing any more water than is necessary. There are also stomata – tiny holes in the cuticle that breathe in carbon dioxide and breathe out oxygen. These allow some water to pass out of the leaf in a process called transpiration.

## The inner leaf

The cells in the leaf contain a green pigment called chlorophyll, which absorbs light and energy from the sun. This energy is used to combine carbon dioxide (from the atmosphere) with water (which the roots absorb from the soil) to produce glucose and oxygen, in a process called photosynthesis. Glucose provides energy to make the tree grow.

*If you cut a leaf in half, this is what the cut edge looks like under the microscope.* ▶

▼ *Some trees are at their most spectacular to look at in the autumn when their leaves lose their green pigment, and red, orange and yellow tones are highly visible.*

### A LEAF'S LIFE CYCLE

In spring new leaves are bright in colour. They turn darker as they age and eventually fade and drop from the tree in autumn.

*Early spring*

*Summer*

*Autumn*

*Winter*

## Leaf shapes

For most trees, the leaves are probably the most important way to identify them. There are six main types of leaf, which are either "simple" with just one leaf on each stalk, or "compound", with more than one leaf, as well as the needles and scales found on conifers.

## Simple leaves

These include:

*Rounded*

*Lobed*

■ entire or whole leaves, which are undivided and have a smooth edge, such as magnolia.
■ serrated leaves, which have teeth (serrations) around the edge, such as plum.
■ lobed leaves, which curve in towards the centre and then back out again, such as oak.
■ palmate leaves, which means hand- or palm-like, with very big serrations, such as the Japanese maple.

*Compound*

*Palmate and serrated*

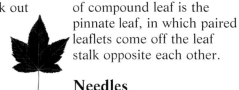

## Compound leaves

The leaflets of compound leaves such as the horse chestnut may look like separate leaves growing off the same stalk, but in fact the whole stalk and its leaflets all emerge from the same bud, meaning that it is in fact just one leaf (known as a compound palmate leaf). Another form of compound leaf is the pinnate leaf, in which paired leaflets come off the leaf stalk opposite each other.

## Needles

*Needles*

Evergreen trees, which include most conifers and trees such as holly, box and laurel, have leaves that fall from the tree and are replaced throughout the year, rather than having a seasonal drop. Most conifers have needle-like leaves. Needles lose less water than leaves of broad-leaved trees, and are better at surviving when water is scarce. A few conifers, such as cypress, juniper and cedar, have small, scale-like leaves.

---

PRESSING LEAVES

**You will need**
gloves, leaves, kitchen paper, heavy books, glue, notebook, pen

1. Start your leaf collection by picking fallen leaves or cut fresh ones. Wear gloves.

2. Place the leaves flat between sheets of kitchen paper and place the leaf sandwich between the pages of a heavy book. Stack more books on top.

3. In one month the leaves will be flat and dry. Glue them to your notebook. Identify each one.

# Flowers and Pollination

*Many tree flowers are very distinct and provide an instant and easy means of identifying a tree. In temperate regions of the world, flowers usually begin to appear on the trees in spring and last for just a few weeks.*

A tree's flowers may appear on the tree before any of its leaves. Usually this occurs in early spring. While the flowers are attractive for us humans to look at, their main purpose is to attract insects and birds to them, so that the flowers will be pollinated and the survival of the tree species is ensured.

Some tree flowers are insignificant to look at, while others are large and colourful, with powerful scents. Their colours and scent make them attractive to different pollinating insects and birds. Once pollinated the flower's petals will fall away and in their place a fruit with the next generation of seeds will develop.

◀ *Boughs of blossom look spectacular in spring when they cover the entire crown of the tree.*

## Inside the flower

Most flowers have four main parts:

■ the stamen, which is the male reproductive organ and produces the pollen

■ the stigma, which receives the pollen

■ the style, which links the stigma to the ovary

■ the ovary, which contains ovules, which, after fertilization, develop into seeds.

When all these parts are in one flower, the flower is said to be "perfect", and the tree can pollinate itself. Examples of trees with "perfect" flowers are cherry, laburnum and lime. Some trees are "male" or "female", so two trees are needed for pollination. In these cases the trees need to be growing closely to have a chance of pollination by insects or wind.

**Stamen**

**Pistil (stigma, style and ovary)**

▼ *Flowers take many forms, from big, frothy open flowers to tiny cones on conifers.*

*Apple blossom*

*Cherry blossom*

*Tulip tree*

*Chinese juniper*

## How are flowers pollinated?

A tree cannot go looking for a partner as we humans do, so it needs something to act as a go-between so that the male parts of the flower can fertilize the female parts. This may be wind or birds, but more commonly it is insects such as bees, wasps and flies. Insects and the wind are the most common pollinators of temperate trees, although a few are pollinated by birds.

## Insects

Most trees are pollinated by insects, such as bees, and they tend to have flowers with lots of sugary-sweet nectar to attract them. Their pollen grains are larger than those of wind-pollinated trees and also quite sticky, so that they adhere to the insects' bodies. Trees that attract insects may use colour and/or scent.

The handkerchief tree, *Davidia involucrata*, for example, has flowers with large white bracts (a kind of leaf) surrounding them to guide pollinating moths to its flowers by night. The flowers of cherry and hawthorn trees have very attractive petals and are scented to guide the insects.

*The white bracts of the handkerchief tree.* ▶

## Wind

All conifers are wind pollinated, and most produce such large amounts of tiny-grained pollen that on breezy days clouds of pollen may fill the air around them. The male flowers containing the pollen-bearing stamens are on the tips of the branches so that it is easy for the pollen to leave the tree. Other wind-pollinated trees, such as alder, birch and hazel, carry their pollen grains in drooping catkins, which appear on the trees earlier than the leaves.

## LIFE CYCLE OF A FLOWER

Although a tree's flowers last just a short time, their life cycle lasts for most of the year. At the end of the cycle when the tree's branches are bare, the buds for next year will already have formed and will be kept protected by the tree until the temperature warms up in the spring. When the growing conditions are right, the buds that the tree kept protected will start to develop into flowers and leaves. The flowers last for a few weeks until they are pollinated by insects, birds or the wind. Once pollinated, the fruit grows in place of the flower. Inside the fruit is a seed (often many seeds) from which another tree can grow, but only if it lands in fertile ground and the growing conditions are right.

*Spring*   *Summer*   *Late summer*   *Autumn*   *Late autumn*

# Seeds and Germination

*Every tree begins life as a tiny seed. Seeds contain all that is necessary for a mature tree to grow. They may be contained within nuts, fruit, berries or cones, or have "wings" so that they can be swept away by the wind or water.*

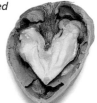

◀ *Sweet chestnuts are protected by a hard, spiky case.*

*Some seeds are contained* ▶ *within a sealed protective shell. Walnuts are held inside a smooth, hard case.*

◀ *Acorns are a valuable food source for animals.*

*Chestnuts* ▶ *in a prickly casing*

Seeds are produced from the female part of the flower (or from the female flower) once it has been pollinated and one or more of its ovules fertilized. There are many different ways in which the seeds can be "wrapped" ready for distribution. Whichever method is used, the aim is the same: to get the seed as far away from the parent plant as possible to increase its chances of survival and reduce competition with the parent.

## Nuts

These are edible seeds and they vary in size and shape. Some, such as hazelnuts, are inside a woody shell. Others, such as chestnuts, are surrounded by an inedible but fleshy outer coating. Squirrels and jays both bury nuts that they are unable to eat straight away. Sometimes they never return to a store, which allows those nuts to germinate, if they have been buried in the nutrient-rich soil.

### GERMINATION OF A SEED

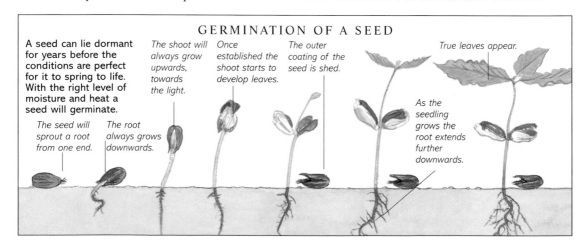

A seed can lie dormant for years before the conditions are perfect for it to spring to life. With the right level of moisture and heat a seed will germinate.

*The seed will sprout a root from one end.*

*The root always grows downwards.*

*The shoot will always grow upwards, towards the light.*

*Once established the shoot starts to develop leaves.*

*The outer coating of the seed is shed.*

*As the seedling grows the root extends further downwards.*

*True leaves appear.*

## Fruit and berries

Some trees wrap their seeds inside brightly coloured, sweet-tasting fruits or berries. The fruit or berry has two roles: first it protects the seed, and second, it tempts animals and birds to eat it. Bright red rowan berries are loved by starlings, while red holly berries attract fieldfares (a type of thrush). Normally the flesh of berries is digested but the seed is not, and it gets passed out in the bird's droppings.

*Berries*

Fruits come in many different sizes and colours, and many are eaten regularly by humans. The seeds are present as pips, in the case of apples, or contained within stones (pits), as in plums. Any pips or stones that end up on the ground have a chance to germinate.

## Dry and oil-coated seeds

Many dry seeds rely on wind for their dispersal. Eucalyptus seed is like fine dust and can be carried considerable distances on the wind. Maple and ash seeds have extended wings, known as "keys", which help to keep them airborne. Alder trees grow near water, and each of their seeds is attached to a tiny

*Key*

drop of oil. After falling from the tree into the water, the seed floats downstream, kept afloat by the oil bubble, until it is washed ashore.

## Cones

Seeds of conifer trees are encased together in a cone, where each seed is often equipped with light, papery wings, which enable it to "fly" away from the parent tree on the wind.

*Cone*

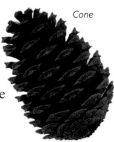

▼ *Seeds can germinate almost anywhere where there is light, water and nutrients.*

### LOOKING AT SEEDS

Seeds are generally small, but each variety looks different. Cut open some fruits and compare them

**You will need**
soft fruit such as apple, orange, nectarine, plum, papaya, cutting board, knife

1. Working on a cutting board, cut open your selection of fruit with a sharp knife. Inside you will find seeds that have grown from a pollinated female flower.

2. Remove the seed (this is an apple seed) from the fruit. Small seeds are often coated with an outer skin. Remove the skin carefully.

# The Life Cycle of a Tree

*The life of a tree is in many cases a very long, process of change and development: from a time of rapid growth, when a sapling, or young tree, establishes itself, through a long period of little change, to a slow decline into old age and death.*

A new tree begins with the germination of a seed. Once the seed has developed tiny roots the process of growth begins. During the first few years the tree is very vulnerable to being damaged by animals or weakened by drought or frost. Once it is established, however, it can get down to some serious growing. Trees grow in three different ways – upwards, downwards and outwards – and the rate of growth depends on how much water and light they receive.

Sunlight in

◀ *Trees need sunlight and water to thrive. Both are needed to create the food sap inside the leaves that keeps the tree alive.*

▲ Water in

Acorn   Young growth

Acorn

◀*The acorn is a small nut from which a huge oak tree will grow. Young growth is very tender and could be eaten by a grazing animal or killed by extreme weather.*

## Upward growth

You might think that if you paint a ring around a tree 2m/6ft above the ground, and then return to it in a few years when the tree has grown, the ring would be higher than 2m/6ft. This is not the case: the ring would stay at the same level. This is because the growth happens at the top of the tree. At the tip of each branch are growing cells. As these divide, they make each branch grow longer, so the tree becomes taller and wider.

▼ *Once established a seedling will continue to grow.*

▼ *It can take hundreds of years for trees to grow to maturity.*

▼ *In old age the tree trunk becomes hollow.*

## MEASURING THE HEIGHT OF A TREE

**You will need**

pencil, stick, tape measure or ruler, notebook

1. Stand in front of the tree. Hold out a pencil at arm's length so that you can see it and the tree at the same time. Ask a friend to stand at the bottom of the tree.

2. Line the pencil up so that the top of it is in line with the top of the tree. Move your thumb down the pencil until it is level with the bottom of the tree. Turn the pencil so that it is horizontal, still keeping your thumb level with the bottom of the tree.

3. Ask your friend to walk away from the tree, then stop when she is level with the top of the pencil. Mark the place where your friend stands with a stick. Measure the distance from the stick to the tree. This distance is the same as the height of the tree.

## Downward growth

There is a direct relationship between the amount of upward growth by the branches and the downward growth by the roots. This is known as the root:shoot ratio. The leaves on the branches provide a sugary food for the whole tree, and in turn the roots provide water and minerals for the leaves. As a tree grows, it produces more leaves. These require more water and minerals, so the root system needs to grow in order to provide these and to anchor the tree in the ground. But in order for the root system to grow, more food is needed from the leaves. And so it goes on. The balance between the leaves and roots is a fine one: if either of them fails, the tree may die.

## Outward growth

As the tree grows taller, the branches grow longer, and the trunk becomes wider. The branches and roots are thicker at the point where they meet the trunk, so that the tree can transport increasing amounts of water and food to and from its branches. In temperate climates, all growth occurs in spring and summer when the weather warms up.

## Old age

As the tree gets older, so its rate of growth slows down and eventually stops. As long as the root:shoot ratio is balanced, the tree can live for many years, but an ageing tree may be attacked by disease, and may start to die.

### GROWTH RINGS

The cycle of growth in a temperate tree can be clearly seen when the tree is cut down. Each year the new cells that are produced under the bark create a new ring of tissue, which has light and dark sections. These rings are known as growth rings. By counting them it is possible to work out the tree's age.

# How to Identify Trees

*Looking at and identifying trees can be very enjoyable and interesting, but, unless you know what to look for, it could also be very confusing. The following information explains what to look for and how to identify any trees you find.*

There are seven main features of a tree that will give you clues to its identity (though these will usually not all be visible at the same time). The seven things to look out for on your checklist are:

## Shape and size
Some trees have a strikingly distinctive shape. Take the chile pine, better known as the monkey puzzle tree, *Araucaria araucana*, for example. No other evergreen tree has such stiff branching, with tips that curl up.

## Evergreen or deciduous
If it is winter time, it will not be hard to see whether the tree has dropped its leaves (in which case it is deciduous) or not (in which case it is evergreen). If it is summer, then you need to look for signs of the three types of evergreen leaf: long, thin and needle-like; short, pointed and scale-like; or thick and leathery, often with a shiny surface.

## Leaves
There are many different leaf shapes, so record as many as you can find.

## Flowers
To identify flowers, you need to ask yourself the following questions. What colour are they? Do they have simple or complex shapes? Are the flowers growing alone or in clusters? Are they on the ends of twigs or in the leaf axils (the point where the leaf joins the stalk)?

## Fruit
This can take many forms: large fleshy fruits, such as apples; smaller nuts, such as chestnuts and acorns; pods, such as those on

▲ *Collecting and recording details are the best methods of learning about trees.*

laburnums; and winged fruits, such as ash keys. The cones produced by conifers have developed from flowers. Each cone contains many seeds.

## Bark
Some trees are probably better known by their bark than any other feature, such as the silver birch (*Betula pendula*), which has striking silver-white bark. With other trees it may be the way the bark has formed cracks or is flaking off that will give you important clues.

## Buds
In winter time, the buds will be a helpful way to identify a tree. Ash trees, for example, have very distinctive black buds, while sycamore buds are lime green. Some buds are smooth and shiny and others have a downy coat.

# COLLECTING SPECIMENS TO DISPLAY

1. How many different types of leaves can you find? Remember to look for different shapes, colours and textures. Are the edges wavy, serrated or smooth? Note down the tree that you take each from. You could make a rubbing from each and then press them.

2. Only collect bark from dead trees that have fallen over; never remove bark from a tree that's alive. However, you can make bark rubbings from many different trees. Look out for lots of different textures. Why not measure the girth of each tree too?

3. You could take photographs of different trees when they are in flower, or cut out photographs from magazines. Flowers only last for a short time, but you could collect any that have fallen from the tree and try and press them. You could also collect nuts, cones and needles.

4. Once you have got together a collection of specimens, you could start to arrange them into a logical collection. Make a display case from a shoe box, and glue your finds into different compartments made from cardboard. Arrange leaf pressings and bark rubbings on paper together with the name of the tree.

# Tree Habitats

*A tree's habitat is its home and every tree has adapted to the conditions in which it lives. Trees that survive by the sea have learnt to cope with salt water, while many conifers have adapted to cold climates.*

## Urban trees

Trees have been planted in large numbers in our towns and cities for centuries. They are beneficial in an urban setting because they reduce air pollution. They do this by trapping dust, ash and smoke (from cars and factories, for example), which can damage human lungs. They also absorb carbon dioxide and other dangerous gases. To put it simply, they clean the air for us. Other benefits of urban trees are that they reduce wind speed around high-rise buildings, offer cooling shade on hot, sunny days, screen ugly buildings, and generally provide a more pleasant place in which to live and work.

## Coastal trees

Strong winds will batter coastal areas at any time of the year. Trees have adapted to these winds by growing extra roots on the windy side, to anchor them into the ground more firmly. Many trees have also changed the way they grow, so that instead of being tall, they grow low and squat, just as we might keep our heads down in a strong wind. The stone pine (*Pinus pinea*), which has developed a very low, domed top to make it wind-resistant, has been planted in coastal regions since Roman times. The trees growing on the west coasts of Britain and Ireland benefit from the Gulf Stream, a warm sea current from the Caribbean. This means that the trees that came from the Mediterranean region can flourish here.

## Forests and woodland

The different forest and woodland trees that grow in Europe can be divided into three separate types: Mediterranean (southern Europe), temperate (central and western Europe) and boreal (northern and eastern Europe). Mediterranean trees enjoy a climate of hot dry summers, and winters with only a little rain. Trees that thrive here include the holm oak (*Quercus ilex*), the Italian cypress (*Cupressus sempervirens*) and the sweet chestnut (*Castanea sativa*).

Temperate trees exist in a damp and windy climate, with cold temperatures in winter. Both deciduous and evergreen trees grow in this climate, but it is mainly deciduous trees, such as oak, beech and birch, which live here.

Boreal trees grow in northerly parts of Europe, which have very long winters, and therefore the trees have short growing seasons. The types of tree to be found here are conifers such as the Scots pine (*Pinus sylvestris*) and the Norway spruce (*Picea abies*). Despite the poor growing conditions, more tree species can be found in this region than in the other two regions.

## Mountain trees

In many ways, mountains have the same climate as the subarctic regions of the world. They have short summers, cold winters and an average temperature that rarely rises above 10°C/50°F. They also have much greater wind speeds and shallow soil, which can be frozen for long periods of time.

To survive in these poor conditions, trees need to be protected against water loss and frost damage, and both conifers and broad-leaved evergreens have leaves that are resistant to both water loss and cold. Many mountain trees are conical (like a cone) or spire-shaped, with branches and twigs that point down. This prevents snow from building up on the branches and breaking them.

# Looking at Conifers

Conifers include pines, yews, cypresses, redwoods, firs, junipers, cedars, spruces and larches. The diverse selection included here thrives throughout Europe. Most of these trees are evergreen and have needle-like leaves, though some have scale-like leaves. These trees produce male and female flowers, which often look like miniature cones, often on separate trees. The female flowers are usually bigger, and when they are fertilized by the pollen from the male flowers, they turn into a fruit – usually a woody cone, but sometimes a berry.

## Chile Pine

Monkey puzzle *Araucaria araucana*

With its long, curling branches and deep green pointed leaves, the Chile pine is a very strange-looking tree. When the tree is young, the branches go right down to the ground, but as it gets older, the lower branches fall off, leaving the ridged grey bark on view. Its common name refers to the idea that monkeys would have difficulty climbing such a spiky tree. In the Andes, where it is from, so many Chile pine forests have been cut down for timber that there are now more of these trees in Britain than there are in South America.

▲ The thick, leathery leaves grow in spirals around the shoot.

### IDENTIFICATION

- The bark is wrinkled and grey, rather like an elephant's skin.
- The dark green leaves are triangular-shaped, sharp and pointed.
- The fruits are male and female cones, which usually grow on separate trees.

*Male cones, like this one, grow at the tips of shoots, whereas female cones grow on the upper sides.*

FACT FILE

**Region of origin** Forms groves in the Andean forests of Chile and south-western Argentina.
**Height** 50m/165ft
**Shape** Broadly conical, becoming domed in maturity
**Evergreen**
**Pollinated** Wind
**Leaf shape** Linear to triangular

# Common Yew

*Taxus baccata*

Many people think that the common yew is a rather gloomy-looking tree. This is partly because the dark leaves and branches grow so closely together that the tree looks quite forbidding, and partly because it has been planted in churchyards for centuries. Yews can live for a very long time, and many are over 1,000 years old. They do not grow very tall, but their canopy can grow to 12m/40ft wide. Such large trees usually have hollow trunks. The wood is used for making furniture. The oldest tree in Europe is the Fortingall yew, in Scotland, which is believed to be at least 4,000 years old.

▲ *Yew leaves are needle-like in appearance. They are poisonous, as are the bark, shoots and seeds.*

**FACT FILE**

**Region of origin**
Europe, eastwards to northern Iran and the Atlas mountains of North Africa.
**Height** 20m/65ft
**Shape** Broadly conical
**Evergreen**
**Pollinated** Wind
**Leaf shape** Linear

*The branches grow very closely together, so there is little light under the tree.*

*A single black seed can be seen at the hollow end of each bright red fruit.*

## IDENTIFICATION

- The bark is rich brown with a purplish tone, and peels away to show reddish patches.

- The thin, pointed leaves are glossy on top and have a groove running down the centre.

- Yellow male cones and green female cones grow on separate trees.

- The fruits are fleshy berries that turn red when they are ripe.

# Sawara Cypress

*Chamaecyparis pisifera*

This tree can reach a height of over 20m/65ft in the wild. Its branches, which sweep upwards, grow in two spreading rows on each side of the trunk, with quite a lot of space in between them. The leaves are a bright shiny green on top, and have two bands of white stomata (breathing holes) underneath. When crushed, they have a strong smell of resin.

The leaves grow in flattened sprays.

## IDENTIFICATION

- The bark is deep reddish-brown, deeply cracked, and peels off in strips.
- The scale-like leaves are bright green on top with bands of white underneath.
- The tiny male flowers are pale brown; the female flowers are green and 5mm/¼in wide.
- The cones are mid-brown and the size of a pea. Each cone has up to 12 scales and is hollow towards the centre.

### FACT FILE

**Region of origin**
Found throughout the Honshu and Kyushu islands of Japan.
**Height** 20m/65ft
**Shape** Conical
**Evergreen**
**Pollinated** Wind
**Leaf shape** Linear scale-like

# Lawson Cypress

Port Orford cedar, Oregon cedar *Chamaecyparis lawsoniana*

The Lawson cypress is tall and thin, with branches that droop at their tips. It has reddish-brown bark and scented leaves, which are thick and leathery. This is a useful tree, because it will grow in any type of soil, can cope with cold weather and rarely gets troubled by pests and diseases. It is a very important source of timber in its native North America, and is used for boat-building and furniture-making.

The cones remain on the tree for a long time after the seeds have been shed.

The cones become woody and wrinkled.

The tops of the leaves are dark green to bluish-green, and smell of parsley when crushed.

## IDENTIFICATION

- The bark is smooth, brown-green and shiny on young trees, but becomes more reddish and cracked.
- The scale-like leaves have a parsley-like smell.
- The cones are round and purple-brown in colour.

▲ **The male flowers are dark red.**

The bark develops long, vertical cracks.

### FACT FILE

**Region of origin** North-western USA from south-west Oregon to north-west California. Present in the Klamath and Siskiyou Mountains to an altitude approaching 2,000m/6,500ft.
**Height** 40m/130ft
**Shape** Narrowly conical
**Evergreen**
**Pollinated** Wind
**Leaf shape** Linear scale-like

# Monterey Cypress

*Cupressus macrocarpa*

This tree has become a common sight along the unprotected coastal areas of Europe. It can grow to 40m/130ft, but trees are often stunted by their exposure to strong, salt-laden winds. The wood is very strong and often used for building work. The Monterey cypress is the female parent of the Leyland cypress (x *Cupressocyparis leylandii*), which is popular for hedges.

*The purplish-brown cones are up to 4cm/1½in across.*

## FACT FILE

**Region of origin**
USA: known from two sites along the coastline near Monterey, California, at Cypress Point and Point Lobos.
**Height** 40m/130ft
**Shape** Broadly conical
**Evergreen**
**Pollinated** Wind
**Leaf shape** Linear scale-like

### IDENTIFICATION

- The bark is greyish-brown, with shallow ridges that become deeper.

- The dark green leaves are short and scale-like and smell of lemons when crushed.

- The tiny male flowers are yellow and ovoid; female flowers are greenish-purple.

- The round, glossy cones grow in clusters.

*The bark begins to peel from the trunk of old trees.*

# Italian Cypress

*Cupressus sempervirens*

This is a fascinating tree because, unlike most other conifers, it stays very slim and pointed throughout its life, making it an easy tree to identify. It is planted at regular intervals on the hills and beside the roads of Tuscany in Italy, and the western Mediterranean, where it can reach a height of 20m/65ft or more. The cones are larger than those of most trees in the *Cupressus* genus, growing to 3.5cm/1¼in, similar to those of the Monterey cypress. They stay on the tree for many years.

*The cones ripen from green, through dark red-brown to grey-brown.*

## FACT FILE

**Region of origin** Mainly a Mediterranean tree with a distribution northwards to Switzerland and east to northern Iran.
**Height** 20m/65ft
**Shape** Very narrowly columnar
**Evergreen**
**Pollinated** Wind
**Leaf shape** Linear scale-like

### IDENTIFICATION

- The ridged bark is mainly grey, with some brown colouring.

- The scale-like leaves are a dull grey-green and have no smell when crushed.

- The cones grow up to 3.5cm/1¼in across and are smooth and shiny.

*The Italian cypress is tall and slender, like a church spire.*

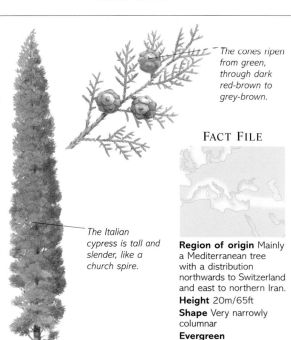

29

# Dawn Redwood

*Metasequoia glyptostroboides*

Until 1941, when this beautiful tree was discovered growing in Szechwan Province in China, it had been seen only as a fossil, and so had been thought to be extinct. It was first introduced to the West in 1948, and since then has become a popular species in parks and gardens. It has a conical shape, with branches that sweep upwards. The top of the tree has lots of branches and leaves when it is grown in the open, but growth is thinner when it is grown in the shade. The bark is bright orange-brown and stringy.

*In autumn, the leaves change to light brown or pinkish-yellow, then to bright red and finally to rust colour.*

*As a deciduous conifer, the dawn redwood loses its leaves in winter.*

*The leaves grow in opposite pairs, not alternately.*

## IDENTIFICATION

- The orange-brown bark has deep grooves in it and peels off older trees in strips.

- The leaves are bright green above, with a greyish-green band on each side of the midrib below. They curve down at the tips.

- The male flowers are ovoid and grow in long clusters towards the tips of the shoots.

- The cones are round to ovoid, have a pointed tip, and hang from a long stalk. They are brown when ripe.

*The trunk is quite often grooved.*

## FACT FILE

**Region of origin** China: the Shui-sha valley, in the north-west part of Hupeh Province and into Szechwan Province.
**Height** 40m/130ft
**Shape** Narrowly conical
**Deciduous**
**Pollinated** Wind
**Leaf shape** Linear

# Douglas Fir

*Pseudotsuga menziesii*

This is one of the most important trees in the world for producing timber. The wood is used for building, fencing, telegraph poles and paper pulp. It is grown throughout North America, Europe, Australia and New Zealand. It is a huge tree, sometimes growing over 75m/245ft tall, and the first branches often do not start until 33m/110ft up the trunk. When the tree is young, it is slender and pointed, but as it gets older, the top becomes flatter. The title of tallest tree in Britain is currently shared between two Douglas firs, both growing in Scotland. Each measures 62m/200ft tall.

▲ The cones have bracts that stick out between the scales. Two winged seeds are produced for each scale.

The branches hang downwards but curve up at the tips.

When crushed, the leaves smell sweet and lemony.

The tall, straight trunk produces very good-quality timber.

The cone hangs down near the tip of the shoot.

## IDENTIFICATION

- The bark is smooth, shiny and greyish-brown on young trees, and deeply ridged, cracked and reddish-brown on older trees.

- The needles have rounded tips and are up to 3cm/1¼in long. They are a rich green above, with two whitish bands of stomata beneath.

- The male flowers are yellow and the female flowers are green, flushed pink to purple.

- The cones grow up to 10cm/4in long, ripening from green to orange-brown.

The bottom of the tree has no branches.

### FACT FILE

**Region of origin**
North-west Pacific Seaboard, from Mexico through USA to Canada, including Vancouver Island.
**Height** 75m/245ft
**Shape** Narrowly conical
**Evergreen**
**Pollinated** Wind
**Leaf shape** Linear

# Chinese Juniper

*Juniperus chinensis*

The Chinese juniper has been cultivated for centuries, and is the most commonly used conifer for bonsai (miniature trees). It grows tall and straight, and has leaves of two different types (scale-like and needle-like) growing on the same shoot. The young, needle-like leaves have two bluish bands on each side of the midrib on top, and are green underneath. The adult, scale-like leaves are dark green on the outer surface and have a broad green stripe on the inner, separated by two white bands of stomata.

## IDENTIFICATION

- The bark is grey to reddish-brown, peeling off in strips.
- New leaves are needle-like and spreading, growing at the base of the shoot.
- The adult leaves are blunt and scale-like, and closely pressed all around the shoot.
- The male flowers are yellow and grow at the tips of the shoots.
- The lumpy round cones are dark purple with a pale-grey coating.

▲ *Yellow male flowers grow on shoot tips.*

*The scale-like older leaves are shown here with some ripening cones.*

*The young leaves are needle-like, long and sharply pointed.*

FACT FILE

**Region of origin** Widely distributed through north and east China. Also present in Inner Mongolia and around Japan, restricted to the coastal areas of Honshu, Kyushu and Shikoku.
**Height** 25m/80ft
**Shape** Narrowly conical
**Evergreen**
**Pollinated** Wind
**Leaf shape** Linear scale-like

# Common Juniper

*Juniperus communis*

This usually grows as a spreading shrub, but sometimes forms a column-like tree, similar to the Chinese juniper above, though reaching only 8m/25ft high. The bark is greyish and peels off in strips. The sharply pointed leaves are greyish-green on the outer surface, with a broad whitish band of stomata on the inside. They are scented and glossy. The male flowers are yellow, and the tiny female flowers ripen into bluish-black berries, which are crushed for flavouring gin.

# Eastern Red Cedar

*Juniperus virginiana*

This is the tallest of all the *Juniperus* trees, and it is grown throughout central and southern Europe. The fact that it grows well in very dry and windy places means that it is useful for wind protection. The wood is a beautiful reddish-brown colour, and its scent, which stays when the wood is dried, is very unpleasant to moths, making the wood ideal for lining chests and cupboards where woollen items may be stored. The wood is also used for pencils. Cedarwood oil, which comes from the small, berry-like cones and the leaves, is used in soaps and perfumes.

▲ *Tiny yellow male flowers grow on the tips of shoots.*

*The top of the tree is shaped rather like a pyramid.*

*Unlike the Chinese juniper, the young, needle-like leaves grow at the tip of the shoot.*

## IDENTIFICATION

- The bark is reddish-brown and peels off in long, thin strips.

- The new leaves, which are needle-like, grow at the tips of the shoots.

- The adult leaves, which are scale-like, are a soft green above and grey-green below.

- The male flowers are small and yellow.

- The berry-like cones are light green in spring and dark silvery blue when ripe.

*The trunk is often grooved and has peeling bark.*

## FACT FILE

**Region of origin**
Eastern and central USA: Great Plains eastwards; south-west Maine to southern Minnesota into the Dakotas and southwards to Nebraska and central Texas; east to Florida and Georgia.
**Height** 30m/100ft
**Shape** Narrowly conical
**Evergreen**
**Pollinated** Wind
**Leaf shape** Linear scale-like

# Corsican Pine

*Pinus nigra* subsp. *laricio*

The trunk of this tree grows straight right to the top, which makes it a good source of timber that is strong and has few knots. It is grown throughout Europe for its timber. Like the Austrian pine, *Pinus nigra*, the Corsican pine has fewer, shorter branches, which grow level rather than sweeping upwards.

## IDENTIFICATION

- The bark is light grey to pink and cracked.
- The buds are conical, sharply pointed and covered with white resin.
- The needles are pale grey-green and twisted, and grow in pairs.
- The male flowers are golden-yellow and grow at the base of the shoot.
- The cones are ovoid and up to 8cm/3in long.

The bark has a ▶ flaked or fissured surface from a young age.

Dull pink female flowers grow on the tips of growing shoots.

The needles are up to 18cm/7in long.

FACT FILE

**Region of origin** Southern Italy and Corsica.
**Height** 40m/130ft
**Shape** Broadly columnar
**Evergreen**
**Pollinated** Wind
**Leaf shape** Linear

# Stone Pine

Umbrella pine *Pinus pinea*

The stone pine is widely planted throughout the Mediterranean for its seeds, which are eaten as nuts. It is also known as the umbrella pine because of its flat-topped, umbrella-like shape. The young leaves are bluish-green, changing to dark green as they age, and are up to 12cm/4½in long.

## IDENTIFICATION

- The bark is grey, with orange cracks running down the trunk.
- The needles are long, forward-facing and grow in pairs.
- The cone is almost round, up to 10cm/4in across, and shiny brown.

The needles of the ▶ stone pine are up to 12cm/4½in long.

The closed cone is almost ovoid and remains tightly closed for three years before opening to reveal its seeds.

The female flower forms on the tip of the shoot.

FACT FILE

**Region of origin** Mediterranean from Portugal to Turkey.
**Height** 20m/65ft
**Shape** Broadly spreading
**Evergreen**
**Pollinated** Wind
**Leaf shape** Linear

# Scots Pine

*Pinus sylvestris*

This is one of the temperate world's most widely grown and popular trees. The Scots pine grows well on dry, sandy soil but will also grow in wet conditions, though more slowly. It produces plenty of seed and can colonize new territory quickly: it is well known as a tree that starts growing on newly cleared ground before other trees begin to move in. Its bark is one of its best-known features. It flakes and peels away on the upper trunk and branches, and is deeply cracked and slightly greyer at the base.

*The male flowers appear at the tips of the shoots; the female flowers turn downwards and change from red flowers into brown cones over three years.*

◀ *Old trees have a high, broadly domed top and large, level but snaking branches.*

*The lower trunk is often branchless, as branches tend to remain only at the top on older trees.*

## IDENTIFICATION

- The bark is grey-green on young trees and a stunning orange-red on adult trees.

- The needles are stiff, twisted and bluish-green, and grow in pairs. They are set in an orange-brown casing and are up to 7cm/2¾in long.

- Male flowers are yellow and female are red; both grow in separate clusters on the same tree.

- The cone is ovoid, 7cm/2¾in long, and green, ripening to brown.

## FACT FILE

**Region of origin**
From Scotland right across northern Europe to the Pacific coast and southwards to the Mediterranean and Turkey.
**Height** 35m/115ft
**Shape** Broadly spreading
**Evergreen**
**Pollinated** Wind
**Leaf shape** Linear

# Western Red Cedar

*Thuja plicata*

The timber of the western red cedar has been used for centuries, and individual living trees have been recorded at over 1,000 years old. Native American Indians used to burn out the trunks to make canoes. Its straight-grained timber is popular for fencing and posts. It is a tall, slender tree, narrowing to a point at the top, and has dark, glossy, scented leaves.

## IDENTIFICATION

- The bark is reddish-brown and cracks into plates.
- The scale-like leaves are dark green and glossy above, with whitish markings beneath, and smell sweet when crushed.
- The cones ripen from green to brown and have up to 12 overlapping scales.

The cones grow on flattened sprays of deep green, scale-like leaves.

The bark is ridged and soft and peels off in strips.

### FACT FILE

**Region of origin**
Originating from the Pacific coastline of North America, it grows from southern Alaska, through British Columbia, southwards to Washington and Oregon and the giant coastal redwood forests of California.
**Height** 50m/165ft
**Shape** Narrowly conical
**Evergreen**
**Pollinated** Wind
**Leaf shape** Linear scale-like

# Hiba

*Thujopsis dolabrata*

There is only one tree in the *Thujopsis* genus, and it differs from those in the related *Thuja* genus in having broader leaves with striking white undersides. In Europe, the hiba is slow to grow and often gets no larger than a dense shrub for the first ten years. As an adult tree, it can be tall, slim and upright or much wider with a conical top. The branches grow very close to the ground.

## IDENTIFICATION

- The bark is red-brown to grey, peeling off into fine strips.
- The scented leaves are yellow-green, glossy and hard with a white stripe underneath.
- The cones are roughly round.

The cones are blue-brown and have 6–8 scales.

The leaves are scale-like, 5mm/¼in long, in flattened sprays.

### FACT FILE

**Region of origin** Japan: from the southern islands of central Honshu, westwards to Shikoku and Kyushu.
**Height** 20m/65ft
**Shape** Broadly conical
**Evergreen**
**Pollinated** Wind
**Leaf shape** Linear scale-like

# European Silver Fir

*Abies alba*

This species is widely planted for timber, and is also used as a Christmas tree in many parts of Europe. The new needles that emerge in spring are an attractive lime green, though they often get burnt by the sun melting late frosts. They have two silver bands of stomata underneath, from which they get their name. The cones are clustered on just a few branches at the top of the tree.

The long cones stand upright and fall apart on the tree, rather than hanging down and then falling off in one piece, like the spruces.

### IDENTIFICATION

- The bark is greyish-brown with shallow pinkish-brown cracks that form scales.
- The flexible needles are shiny green above, with silvery-white bands of stomata below.
- The male flowers are small and yellow.
- The cones are red-brown, cylindrical and up to 15cm/6in long.

The needles have silver bands underneath and rounded tips.

### FACT FILE

**Region of origin**
Pyrenees, France, Corsica, the Alps, and the Black Forest to the Balkans.
**Height** 50m/165ft
**Shape** Narrowly conical
**Evergreen**
**Pollinated** Wind
**Leaf shape** Linear

# Noble Fir

*Abies procera*

This is a superb species that truly deserves its name. It has a stately appearance, with a long, straight trunk and large cones (up to 25cm/10in long) that stand proudly above the leaves. Young trees are conical, but older ones become flat-topped. The needles curve upwards from the shoot, then turn down. When crushed, they have a strong smell, like cat's urine.

Female flowers grow upright on the tips of the shoots.

### FACT FILE

### IDENTIFICATION

- The bark is silvery-grey and smooth.
- The needles are grey-green with silvery bands below.
- The male flowers are bright crimson; the female are tall and yellowish green.
- The cones are brown.

Cones fall apart on the tree to leave a central spine.

**Region of origin**
USA: Cascade Mountains of Oregon, Washington State and northern California.
**Height** 80m/260ft
**Shape** Narrowly conical
**Evergreen**
**Pollinated** Wind
**Leaf shape** Linear

# Norway Spruce

*Picea abies*

The Norway spruce is the Christmas tree of Europe. It has a regular, symmetrical form, with horizontal branches at low levels, which gradually turn upwards towards the top of the tree. It grows naturally throughout northern Europe (except for the UK, where it is cultivated) up to altitudes of 1,500m/ 5,000ft. The needles, which are a rich dark green, emit a lemon smell when crushed. The wood is used to make the bellies of violins and other stringed instruments.

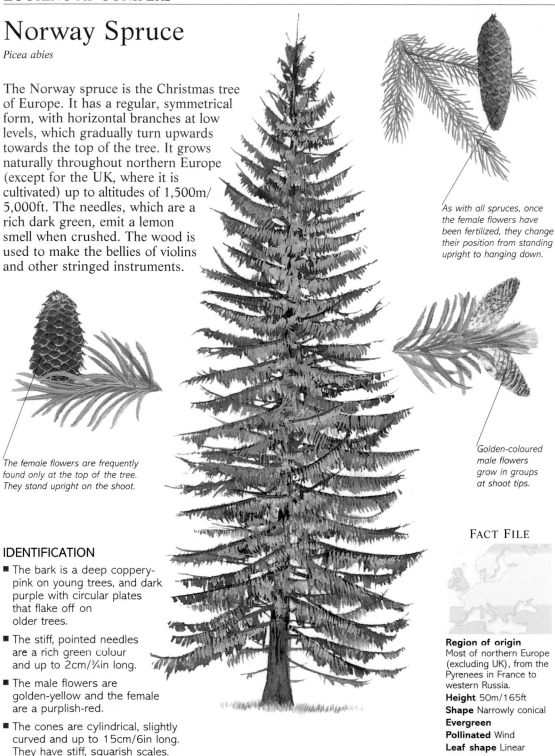

*As with all spruces, once the female flowers have been fertilized, they change their position from standing upright to hanging down.*

*The female flowers are frequently found only at the top of the tree. They stand upright on the shoot.*

*Golden-coloured male flowers grow in groups at shoot tips.*

## IDENTIFICATION

- The bark is a deep coppery-pink on young trees, and dark purple with circular plates that flake off on older trees.

- The stiff, pointed needles are a rich green colour and up to 2cm/¾in long.

- The male flowers are golden-yellow and the female are a purplish-red.

- The cones are cylindrical, slightly curved and up to 15cm/6in long. They have stiff, squarish scales.

## FACT FILE

**Region of origin**
Most of northern Europe (excluding UK), from the Pyrenees in France to western Russia.
**Height** 50m/165ft
**Shape** Narrowly conical
**Evergreen**
**Pollinated** Wind
**Leaf shape** Linear

# Brewer Spruce

*Picea breweriana*

The Brewer spruce is one of the most beautiful conifers. Curtains of ribbon-like leaves hang from evenly spaced, slender branches that arch downwards. The needles are soft and positioned all around the shoot, pointing forwards. Their glossy green surface dulls with age. The male flowers grow on the tips of the shoots, while the female flowers, and therefore the cones, are found only on the topmost branches.

## IDENTIFICATION

- The bark is dark grey-pink on young trees, and purple-grey with circular plates that flake away on older trees.
- The needles are glossy dark green on top with bright white bands of stomata below.
- The male flowers are yellow and red and the female flowers are dark red.
- The cones are light red-brown and cylindrical.

The cones are up to 12cm/4½in long and have rounded edges to their scales.

FACT FILE

**Region of origin** USA: the Siskiyou and Shasta Mountains bordering Oregon and California
**Height** 35m/115ft
**Shape** Narrowly weeping
**Evergreen**
**Pollinated** Wind
**Leaf shape** Linear

# Serbian Spruce

*Picea omorika*

The Serbian spruce is a beautiful, slender, spire-like tree, with branches that sweep elegantly downwards only to arch upwards at their tip. This form of growth means that it is able to resist damage from snow by shedding it rather than collecting it. Like other spruces, its needles are set into little woody pegs, and its cones, found only on the upper branches, hang downwards and may fall to the ground in one piece.

## IDENTIFICATION

- The bark is orange-brown to copper and broken into squarish plates.
- The needles are short with a blunt tip. They are glossy dark green above, with two white bands of stomata below.
- The male and female flowers are both red.
- The cones are purple-brown and tear-shaped.

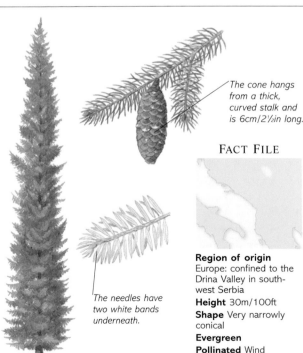

The cone hangs from a thick, curved stalk and is 6cm/2½in long.

FACT FILE

The needles have two white bands underneath.

**Region of origin** Europe: confined to the Drina Valley in south-west Serbia
**Height** 30m/100ft
**Shape** Very narrowly conical
**Evergreen**
**Pollinated** Wind
**Leaf shape** Linear

39

# Colorado Spruce

Blue spruce *Picea pungens*

The Colorado spruce, also known as the blue spruce because of its blue-green needles, grows at heights of up to 3,000m/10,000ft in its native Rocky Mountains. It is often found growing alone on dry slopes and beside dried-up stream beds. It was first discovered in 1862 on Pike's Peak, Colorado. Its sharply pointed needles are a very attractive colour and grow all around the shoot. The male and female flowers appear in separate clusters on the same tree.

## IDENTIFICATION

- The dark red bark is rough with scales.

- The needles are an attractive blue-grey to grey-green, with a slight whitish coating.

- The male flowers are reddish and the female flowers are green.

- The cones are pale brown to cream and up to 10cm/4in long.

The hanging cone, which is cylindrical in shape, has thin scales that are wrinkled at the edges.

### FACT FILE

**Region of origin** USA: Montana, Colorado, Utah, Arizona and New Mexico.
**Height** 35m/115ft
**Shape** Narrowly conical
**Evergreen**
**Pollinated** Wind
**Leaf shape** Linear

# Sitka Spruce

*Picea sitchensis*

This is the largest of the North American spruces, and is widely planted across the Northern Hemisphere in forestry plantations. Its timber is strong yet light. This is the major species used for paper pulp. It is shaped like a narrow cone, with widely spaced branches that point upwards. The tree can easily grow more than 1m/3ft a year when young. The cones have thin, papery scales.

## IDENTIFICATION

- The bark is a deep purple-brown in young trees, developing large cracks.

- The needles are blue-green above with two white bands of stomata beneath.

- The male flowers are reddish and the female are greenish-red.

- The cones are pale buff and 10cm/4in long.

The needles ▶ are stiff with sharp points.

### FACT FILE

**Region of origin** A narrow coastal strip from Kodiak Island, Alaska, to Mendocino County, California.
**Height** 50m/165ft
**Shape** Narrowly conical
**Evergreen**
**Pollinated** Wind
**Leaf shape** Linear

The upright female flowers develop into hanging cones on the uppermost branches.

# Cedar of Lebanon

*Cedrus libani*

*Adult trees have a spreading top that is almost flat and branches that are long and level.*

This large, stately tree is probably the best known of all the cedars. It has been respected for thousands of years and in biblical times it stood as a symbol for fertility. King Solomon used cedar wood from Lebanon, to build the temple in Jerusalem. On Mount Lebanon it grows at heights of up to 1,140m/7,000ft. Its numbers are decreasing in the wild, but it is widely planted in gardens, parks and grave-yards across Europe. For the first 40 years of its life, cedar of Lebanon is a narrow, conical-shaped tree, then it quickly broadens.

*The cones stand upright on the branches and measure 12cm/ 4¾in long.*

## IDENTIFICATION

- The bark is a dull brown with even, narrow cracks.

- The needles are grey-blue to dark green, depending on where the tree is growing, and 3cm/1¼in long. They grow in bunches of 10–20.

- The male flowers are grey-green and up to 5cm/2in long. The female flowers are green then purple, and 1cm/½in long.

- The cone is barrel-shaped and purplish-brown. It has flat scales with purple edges, and a hollow tip.

*The greyish-brown bark develops deep cracks.*

## FACT FILE

**Region of origin** Mount Lebanon, Syria and the Taurus Mountains in south-east Turkey.
**Height** 40m/130ft
**Shape** Broadly columnar
**Evergreen**
**Pollinated** Wind
**Leaf shape** Linear

41

# European Larch

*Larix decidua*

This attractive, hardy tree grows naturally at heights of up to 2,500m/8,200ft. It is a long-lived conifer, with some trees in the Alps recorded at over 700 years old. The European larch has been widely planted throughout Europe and North America for forestry and ornamental reasons. Its timber is used for fencing, staircases and telegraph poles. The soft needles grow in bunches of 30–40.

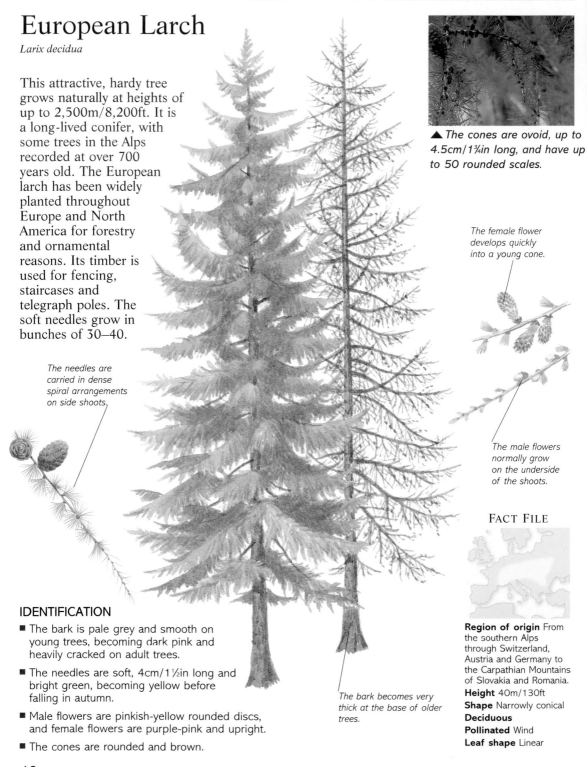

▲ The cones are ovoid, up to 4.5cm/1¾in long, and have up to 50 rounded scales.

The needles are carried in dense spiral arrangements on side shoots.

The female flower develops quickly into a young cone.

The male flowers normally grow on the underside of the shoots.

## IDENTIFICATION

- The bark is pale grey and smooth on young trees, becoming dark pink and heavily cracked on adult trees.

- The needles are soft, 4cm/1½in long and bright green, becoming yellow before falling in autumn.

- Male flowers are pinkish-yellow rounded discs, and female flowers are purple-pink and upright.

- The cones are rounded and brown.

The bark becomes very thick at the base of older trees.

## FACT FILE

**Region of origin** From the southern Alps through Switzerland, Austria and Germany to the Carpathian Mountains of Slovakia and Romania.

**Height** 40m/130ft

**Shape** Narrowly conical

**Deciduous**

**Pollinated** Wind

**Leaf shape** Linear

# Japanese Larch

*Larix kaempferi*

In the wild, the Japanese larch grows only on the volcanic mountains of the Japanese island of Honshu, where it grows at altitudes of over 2,750m/ 9,000ft. It is wider than the European larch. The branches sweep upwards when young, becoming level or even pointing slightly down on older trees. The shoots are purple-red, sometimes with a silvery coating. In Japan, this tree is often trained as a bonsai, as well as being widely planted in forests. In north-western Europe, it is commonly planted for timber and also found in parks and gardens.

▲ Cones are borne at irregular intervals along the shoot.

The needles turn orange before falling in autumn.

Japanese larch cones have scales that turn outwards.

## IDENTIFICATION

- The bark is red-brown and scaly.

- The needles are 5cm/2in long, and flatter and broader than those of the European larch. They dull to grey-green in summer.

- Male flowers are yellow globules clustered on hanging shoots. Female flowers, which occur all over the tree, have a pink centre and creamy-yellow margins.

- The cones are round to bun-shaped and 3cm/1¼in long, with outward-turning scales.

## FACT FILE

**Region of origin**
Central Honshu, Japan.
**Height** 30m/100ft
**Shape** Broadly conical
**Deciduous**
**Pollinated** Wind
**Leaf shape** Linear

# Interesting Leaves

Tree leaves come in all shapes and sizes, and many are fairly ordinary. Some trees, however, have leaves that are special in some way, and these are the ones included here. The bay laurel has leaves that are used as a herb to flavour food, while the katsura has leaves that smell of toffee. The box has leaves that are ideal for clipping into shapes. The weeping willow's leaves fall in curtains down to the water, and those of the whitebeam provide a sight of flickering green and white as they move with the wind. The aspen's leaves tremble in the breeze, and the maples offer outstanding autumn colours.

## Bay Laurel

Sweet bay *Laurus nobilis*

This is the laurel used by the ancient Greeks and Romans as a ceremonial symbol of victory. It was usually woven into crowns to be worn by champions. It is a thickly growing small tree or shrub with scented leaves that are often used as food flavouring. The leaves, which have wavy edges and are pointed at the tip, are picked, then left to dry, after which they can be stored for long periods. The male flowers appear in late winter, growing in the axils of last year's leaves.

### IDENTIFICATION

- The bark is dark grey and smooth, becoming cracked.

- The evergreen leaves are leathery, 10cm/4in long, with crinkled edges and dark red stalks.

- The male flowers are greenish-yellow with many yellow stamens. The female flowers are whitish-yellow and on separate trees.

- The fruits are rounded berries, which ripen from green to glossy black.

*The trunk often divides into several stems. The branches sweep upwards.*

▲ *The small male flowers open during late winter.*

*The fruit is a rounded berry, 1cm/½in across.*

### FACT FILE

**Region of origin**
Mediterranean.
**Height** 15m/50ft
**Shape** Broadly conical
**Evergreen**
**Pollinated** Insect
**Leaf shape** Elliptic

# Common Box

*Buxus sempervirens*

This small tree or spreading shrub, which clips well, has been grown for centuries in gardens for hedging, screening and topiary. Its leaves are rounded at the tip, with a distinctive notch. The wood is used for rulers and shaped into chess pieces and sculptures.

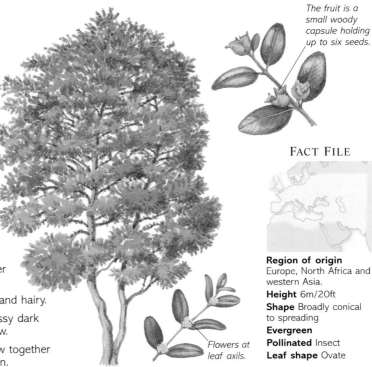

The fruit is a small woody capsule holding up to six seeds.

## IDENTIFICATION

- The bark is fawn and smooth, later cracking into tiny plates.
- The buds are pale orange-brown and hairy.
- The leaves are long and oval, glossy dark green above and pale green below.
- The male and female flowers grow together in clusters and are yellowish-green.

Flowers at leaf axils.

## FACT FILE

**Region of origin**
Europe, North Africa and western Asia.
**Height** 6m/20ft
**Shape** Broadly conical to spreading
**Evergreen**
**Pollinated** Insect
**Leaf shape** Ovate

# Katsura Tree

*Cercidiphyllum japonicum*

This graceful tree, with its slender, curving branches, is popular in gardens and parks. Its attractive leaves have a smell of toffee when they begin to rot. Once it is securely growing, it may grow by 60cm/2ft a year.

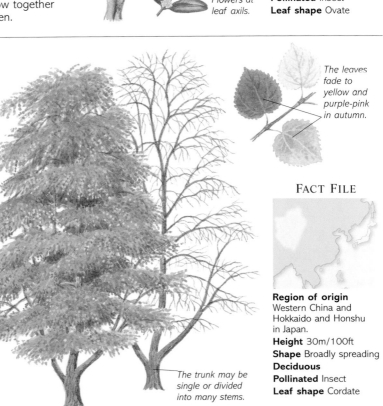

The leaves fade to yellow and purple-pink in autumn.

## IDENTIFICATION

- The bark is grey-brown, becoming cracked.
- The buds are dark brown.
- The leaves are heart-shaped, with small teeth around the edges.
- The male and female flowers grow on separate trees.

The trunk may be single or divided into many stems.

## FACT FILE

**Region of origin**
Western China and Hokkaido and Honshu in Japan.
**Height** 30m/100ft
**Shape** Broadly spreading
**Deciduous**
**Pollinated** Insect
**Leaf shape** Cordate

# Caucasian Elm

*Zelkova carpinifolia*

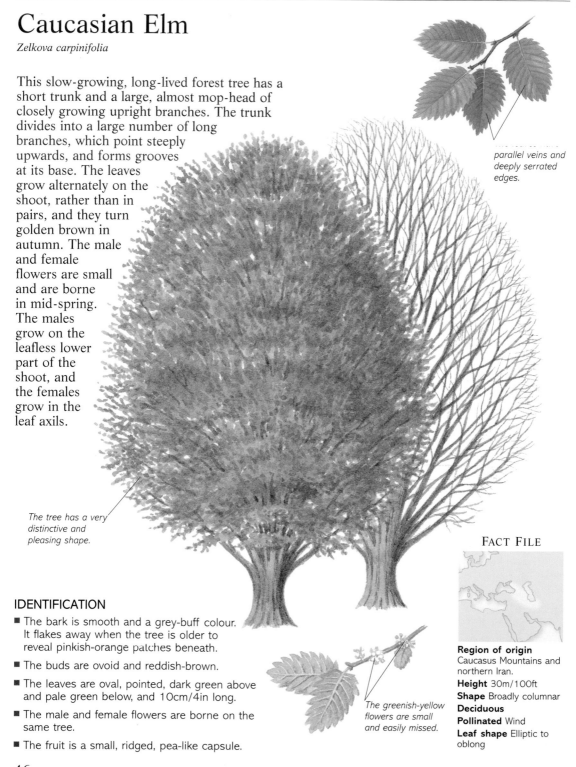

This slow-growing, long-lived forest tree has a short trunk and a large, almost mop-head of closely growing upright branches. The trunk divides into a large number of long branches, which point steeply upwards, and forms grooves at its base. The leaves grow alternately on the shoot, rather than in pairs, and they turn golden brown in autumn. The male and female flowers are small and are borne in mid-spring. The males grow on the leafless lower part of the shoot, and the females grow in the leaf axils.

*parallel veins and deeply serrated edges.*

*The tree has a very distinctive and pleasing shape.*

## IDENTIFICATION

- The bark is smooth and a grey-buff colour. It flakes away when the tree is older to reveal pinkish-orange patches beneath.

- The buds are ovoid and reddish-brown.

- The leaves are oval, pointed, dark green above and pale green below, and 10cm/4in long.

- The male and female flowers are borne on the same tree.

- The fruit is a small, ridged, pea-like capsule.

*The greenish-yellow flowers are small and easily missed.*

### FACT FILE

**Region of origin**
Caucasus Mountains and northern Iran.
**Height** 30m/100ft
**Shape** Broadly columnar
**Deciduous**
**Pollinated** Wind
**Leaf shape** Elliptic to oblong

# Keaki

*Zelkova serrata*

This is a large tree that has the general appearance of an elm tree and a similar leaf shape. It can cope with a wide variety of growing conditions: in its native habitat, it can be found in low-lying river valleys, where the soil is deep and rich, as well as in the mountains at heights of up to 1,200m/4,000ft. Many of the oldest Japanese temples are built of its timber, which is strong and long-lasting. It is also beautifully grained, making it suitable for use in high-quality furniture. Its leaves turn pink, yellow and orange in autumn.

*The leaves are more pointed than those of the Caucasian elm.*

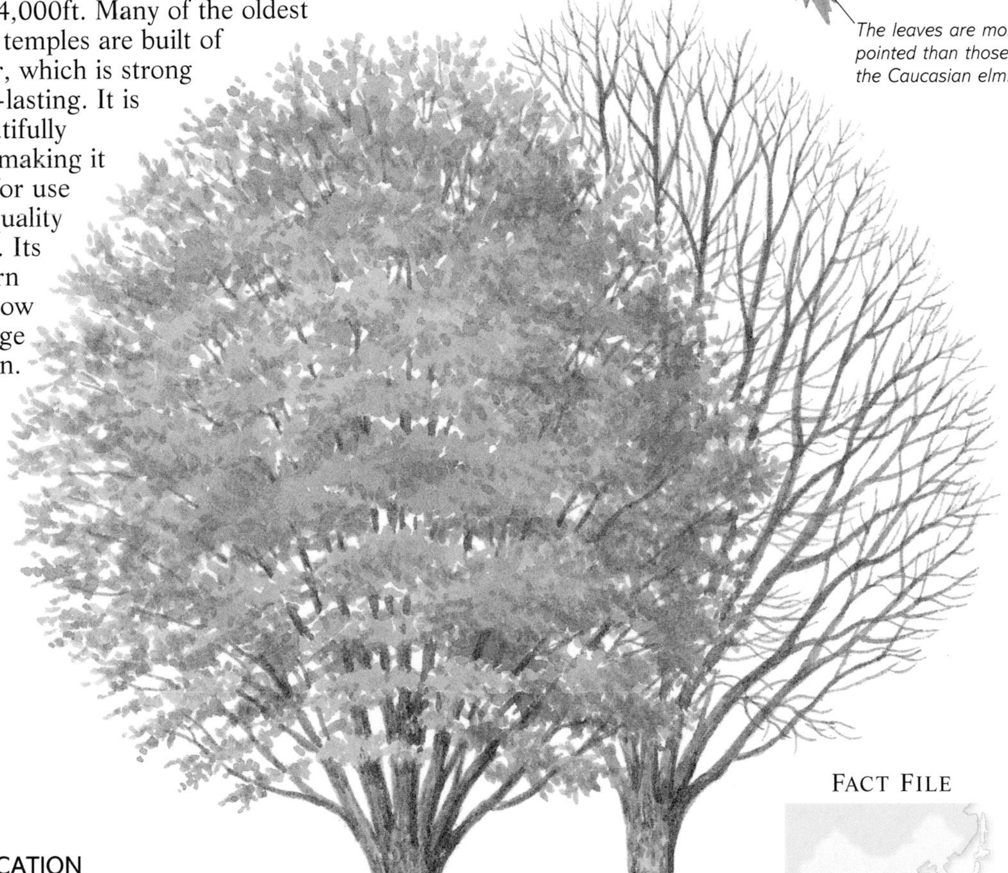

## IDENTIFICATION

- The bark is pale grey and smooth, like beech, peeling to reveal lighter patches.

- The buds are tiny, dark red and ovoid.

- The leaves are dark green and slightly rough above; pale green and hairy beneath.

- The flowers, both male and female, are small and green and appear on the same tree in spring.

- The smooth and rounded fruit grows at the leaf axils.

*In autumn, the leaves turn an orange-red colour.*

## FACT FILE

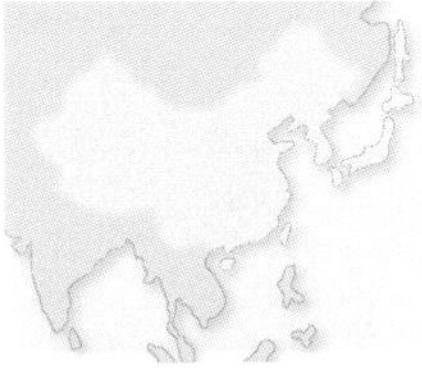

**Region of origin**
China, Japan and Korea.
**Height** 40m/130ft
**Shape** Broadly spreading
**Deciduous**
**Pollinated** Wind
**Leaf shape** Ovate

47

# Common Beech

*Fagus sylvatica*

The beech is a majestic tree, with a beautiful domed shape. It is widely used for hedging because, when clipped, its dead leaves (now orange-brown) stay on the branches in winter, so giving wind protection to the area enclosed by the hedge. The wood is used for furniture.

The leaves have wavy edges, a blunt point at the tip and well-marked veins.

## IDENTIFICATION

- The bark is silver-grey and smooth.
- The slim buds are red-brown and pointed.
- The flowers are borne in separate clusters on the same tree; the males are on long stalks.
- The leaves are dark green and oval.

The husks open in early autumn to reveal the fruit, which is up to three edible nuts.

### FACT FILE

**Region of origin** Europe from the Pyrenees to the Caucasus and north to Russia and Denmark.
**Height** 40m/130ft
**Shape** Broadly spreading
**Deciduous**
**Pollinated** Wind
**Leaf shape** Ovate to obovate

---

# Dawyck Beech

*Fagus sylvatica* 'Dawyck'

This tree was discovered in 1860 on the Dawyck Estate in Scotland. It stood out from the rest of the beech woodland because it was tall and thin, rather than having the spreading shape of the common beech. It became an immediate success with many gardeners, because it provided the perfect solution for those who wanted a beech tree but did not have the space. The leaves are a brighter green than those of the common beech.

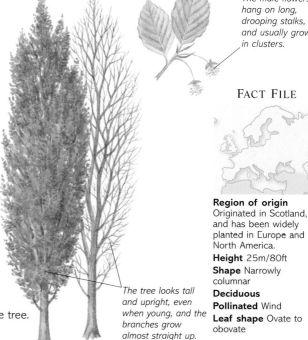

The male flowers hang on long, drooping stalks, and usually grow in clusters.

### FACT FILE

**Region of origin** Originated in Scotland, and has been widely planted in Europe and North America.
**Height** 25m/80ft
**Shape** Narrowly columnar
**Deciduous**
**Pollinated** Wind
**Leaf shape** Ovate to obovate

The tree looks tall and upright, even when young, and the branches grow almost straight up.

## IDENTIFICATION

- The bark is thin and grey.
- The buds are cigar-shaped and red-brown.
- Leaves are bright green, turning bronze.
- Male and female flowers appear on the same tree.
- The fruit is an edible nut in a woody husk.

# Persian Ironwood

*Parrotia persica*

When this tree grows in the wild, it tends to be a wide, upright tree, but in cultivation it becomes a sprawling mass, rarely growing taller than 15m/50ft, with criss-cross branches. The leaves are oval, 12cm/4¾in long, and become more shallow-toothed and wavy towards the tip of each leaf. The crowded clusters of tiny flowers are clothed in a velvety-soft brown casing and emerge in a startling ruby-red colour, which stands out dramatically on the bare branches in midwinter.

▲ *The leaves have some of the finest autumn colours, turning golden and copper then deep purple-brown.*

*The leaves are dark and glossy on top, and lighter beneath.*

## IDENTIFICATION

- The bark is dark brown, flaking to reveal lighter patches.

- The buds are dark purple and hairy.

- The leaves are bright glossy green above, and dull green and slightly hairy below.

- The flowers are tiny, bright red and grow in short-stalked clusters.

- The fruit is a nut-like brown capsule, 1cm/½in across.

*Small ruby-red flowers appear in winter.*

## FACT FILE

**Region of origin** Mount Ararat, eastern Caucasus to northern Iran.
**Height** 20m/65ft
**Shape** Broadly spreading
**Deciduous**
**Pollinated** Insect
**Leaf shape** Obovate

# Weeping Willow

*Salix* x *sepulcralis* 'Chrysocoma'

The weeping willow is a hybrid (mixture) between two other willows: the white willow and the Chinese weeping willow. It developed naturally where these two species began to grow together in western Asia. The form 'Chrysocoma' has been selected and cultivated for its golden shoots and very graceful weeping habit. It is a familiar sight growing along European riverbanks. It is a large, spreading tree, whose main branches grow upwards but whose secondary branches (the branches that grow off the main ones) reach down to the ground. The new wood is golden-yellow, as are the buds. The seed germinates only in damp soil, and so willows spread naturally only near rivers or on marshland.

▲ *The hanging branches of the weeping willow give it an unmistakable shape.*

## IDENTIFICATION

- The bark is pale grey-brown with narrow cracks.

- The buds are bright yellow, long and slender.

- The leaves are mid-green above, much paler beneath, and thinly covered with hairs.

- The flowers are catkins: the males are golden yellow and the females silvery-green. They are borne on separate trees.

*The leaves are long and slender, maturing from yellow-green to mid-green.*

### FACT FILE

**Region of origin** A hybrid, so not native to anywhere, but widely cultivated throughout temperate regions of the world as an ornamental.

**Height** 20m/65ft

**Shape** Broadly weeping

**Deciduous**

**Pollinated** Insect, and occasionally wind

**Leaf shape** Narrowly lanceolate

# White Willow

*Salix alba*

The white willow thrives in damp soils and grows naturally along rivers and in water meadows. Its leaves are lance-like and up to 10cm/4in long. Their silvery undersides show when the leaves are tossed by the wind. A variety of white willow, *Salix caerulea*, has been grown since the early 1700s to make cricket bats.

The male catkins curve upwards. The slender leaves move easily in the wind.

The female catkins become white with seed.

## IDENTIFICATION

- The bark is brown-grey, later cracked.
- The buds are reddish-grey with a curved tip.
- The leaves are grey-green, with silver hairs underneath.
- The flowers are catkins.

### FACT FILE

**Region of origin**
Europe and western Asia.
**Height** 25m/80ft
**Shape** Broadly columnar
**Deciduous**
**Pollinated** Insect, and occasionally wind
**Leaf shape** Lanceolate

# Violet Willow

*Salix daphnoides*

The name "violet willow" refers to the fact that the young shoots of this tree are a striking plum colour, covered with a silvery coating which wears off as the shoot grows. The leaves are shiny dark green above and whitish underneath. In the wild, this hardy tree grows on upland slopes.

The leaves are shiny dark green above, paler below.

Male catkins are bright silvery-yellow.

## IDENTIFICATION

- The bark is grey and smooth.
- The leaves are narrow, tapering at both ends, and have wavy edges with little teeth.
- The flowers are small, silky catkins.
- The fruit is a small green capsule.

### FACT FILE

**Region of origin**
Central Europe from Scandinavia to the Alps, through Asia to the Himalayas and the Urals.
**Height** 10m/30ft
**Shape** Broadly conical
**Deciduous**
**Pollinated** Insect and wind
**Leaf shape** Narrowly elliptic

# Scarlet Oak

*Quercus coccinea*

The scarlet oak is one of the most
attractive trees of eastern North
America, where it comes from.
It contributes greatly to the
autumn leaf-colour
spectacular. The leaves stay
on the trees far longer
than those of any other
autumn-colour trees, and
turn deep red. The leaves
are eaten into by several
angular lobes, some cutting
almost to the midrib.
Each lobe point is tipped
with a sharp bristle.

The leaves have
a very ragged
appearance for
an oak.

The acorns grow
in deep cups.

### FACT FILE

**Region of origin**
Eastern North America
from Ontario to Missouri,
but not Florida.
**Height** 25m/80ft
**Shape** Broadly spreading
**Deciduous**
**Pollinated** Wind
**Leaf shape** Elliptic

## IDENTIFICATION

- The bark is slate-grey and
  smooth, becoming cracked.
- The buds grow in clusters.
- The leaves are dark green and
  glossy, with pale green undersides.
- The male flowers are yellow catkins; the
  females are tiny, borne on the same tree.
- The fruit is an acorn in a deep, shiny cup.

The tree has an
open look due to
the branches being
well spread out.

# Holm Oak

*Quercus ilex*

This domed, densely branched oak tree is
one of the most important trees for shelter in
coastal areas throughout Europe. In the wild
it grows from sea level to altitudes of above
1,500m/5,000ft in Italy, France and Spain.
The bark is charcoal-grey, smooth at first but
quickly developing shallow cracks. The leaves
are up to 10cm/4in long, and, unlike most
oak trees, have no lobes. They are a dull dark
yellow when young, later turning very dark
green with a greyish-green underside.

# Snowy Mespilus

June berry, Serviceberry *Amelanchier lamarckii*

This beautiful little tree is hardy, easy to grow and provides colour from early spring to mid-autumn. Although it has been cultivated in Europe for at least 300 years, some botanists believe that it originally came from Canada. The tree is multi-stemmed and the branches point upwards. The leaves emerge from the bud in early spring, a copper-khaki colour with a covering of silky white hairs on the underside.

*The small black fruits are sweet to taste.*

## IDENTIFICATION

- The bark is smooth and grey, developing cracks later.

- The buds are ovoid, singular and dark brown.

- The leaves turn from copper colour to dark green as the days get gradually warmer. In autumn, they turn red and orange before falling.

- The flowers are white and narrow-petalled, and are borne in upright clusters of 8–10 in early spring.

- The fruit is small and black.

*The white flowers are star-shaped.*

*The leaves are up to 7.5cm/3in long, slightly toothed and attached to the shoot by a 2.5cm/1in-long leaf stalk.*

## FACT FILE

**Region of origin** Naturalized in western Europe. Some people think that it originates from North America.
**Height** 12m/40ft
**Shape** Broadly spreading
**Deciduous**
**Pollinated** Insect
**Leaf shape** Elliptic or ovate

# Kohuho

*Pittosporum tenuifolium*

This bright-leaved evergreen tree has dark grey to black bark on the trunk, branches and shoots. The contrast of black twigs and shoots against light green leaves is extremely attractive and much in demand by florists and flower arrangers. The flowers, which are deep purple, tubular and very small, make up for what they lack in size with a honey-sweet fragrance that can fill a garden on a warm evening in late spring.

## IDENTIFICATION

- The bark is dark grey to black.
- The leaves are light green, 7.5cm/3in long and have a wavy edge.
- The flowers are deep purple and smell of honey.
- The fruit is a brown-black round capsule.

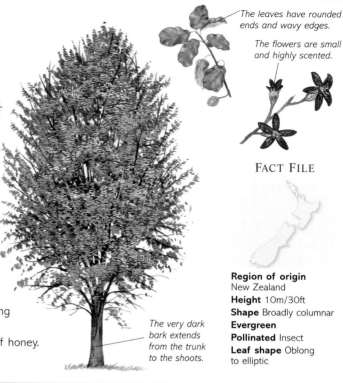

*The leaves have rounded ends and wavy edges.*

*The flowers are small and highly scented.*

### FACT FILE

**Region of origin**
New Zealand
**Height** 10m/30ft
**Shape** Broadly columnar
**Evergreen**
**Pollinated** Insect
**Leaf shape** Oblong to elliptic

*The very dark bark extends from the trunk to the shoots.*

---

# Weeping Silver-leaved Pear

Willow-leaved pear *Pyrus salicifolia*

This tree is the most attractive of all the pears. It is a firm favourite for planting where a small tree with silver leaves is required. The leaves have a characteristic twist along their length. When young, they are covered with silvery-white hair.

## IDENTIFICATION

- The bark is pale grey.
- The buds are densely bunched.
- The leaves are narrow and taper at both ends.
- The flowers are creamy-white with purple anthers.
- The fruit is green and pear-shaped.

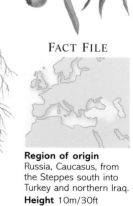

*The flowers grow in clusters, later turning into green fruit.*

### FACT FILE

**Region of origin**
Russia, Caucasus, from the Steppes south into Turkey and northern Iraq.
**Height** 10m/30ft
**Shape** Broadly weeping
**Deciduous**
**Pollinated** Insect
**Leaf shape** Lanceolate

*The bark becomes cracked when the tree gets older.*

# Whitebeam

*Sorbus aria*

By far the most distinguishing feature of this tree is its two-coloured leaves. They are up to 13cm/5in long, pale green when emerging from the bud, and turn a shiny deep green above and white with hairs beneath. When the wind catches the leaves, the effect of flickering green and white over the whole tree is quite remarkable. Although the leaves do not produce good autumn colour, they stay beneath the tree as a grey, crisp covering right through winter.

*The underside of the leaf is white with hair, which contrasts with the deep green top.*

## IDENTIFICATION

- The bark is smooth and silver-grey, developing cracks and ridges.

- The buds are ovoid.

- The leaves are oval, green and white and irregularly toothed.

- The heavily scented flowers are creamy-white and borne in clusters.

- The fruit is a bright red berry, slightly speckled and rough.

*The fruit is made into jam, jelly and wine in some parts of Europe.*

## FACT FILE

**Region of origin** North, west and central Europe.
**Height** 15m/50ft
**Shape** Broadly columnar
**Deciduous**
**Pollinated** Insect
**Leaf shape** Ovate

# Cider Gum

*Eucalyptus gunnii*

This is one of the hardiest of all the eucalyptus species and one of the most widely planted around the world. It has attractive, whitish-blue, rounded young leaves, much prized by florists. The adult leaves are long and slender, and hang from the branches. It also has attractive peeling bark. The cider gum gets its name from the fact that its leaves smell of cider when crushed.

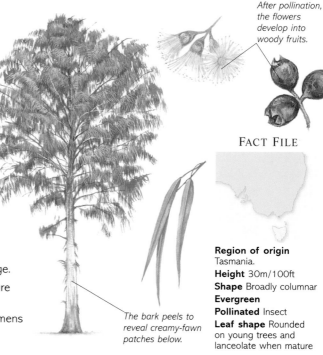

After pollination, the flowers develop into woody fruits.

## IDENTIFICATION

- The bark is smooth and grey-green to orange.
- Young growth has small, round leaves; mature growth has long, narrow, pointed leaves.
- The flowers are white with many yellow stamens and grow in clusters of three.
- The fruit is a green, woody capsule.

The bark peels to reveal creamy-fawn patches below.

**FACT FILE**

**Region of origin**
Tasmania.
**Height** 30m/100ft
**Shape** Broadly columnar
**Evergreen**
**Pollinated** Insect
**Leaf shape** Rounded on young trees and lanceolate when mature

# Tupelo

Black gum, Sour gum *Nyssa sylvatica*

This slow-growing, medium-sized tree is very popular for its spectacular autumn leaf colouring, which ranges from yellow and orange through to red and purple. Male and female flowers are borne in long-stalked clusters on the same tree in summer.

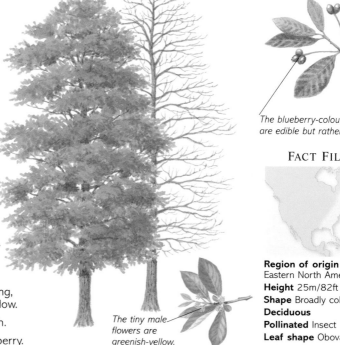

The blueberry-coloured fruits are edible but rather sour.

## IDENTIFICATION

- The bark is dark grey and cracked.
- The buds are reddish-brown and pointed.
- The leaves are up to 15cm/6in long, grass-green above and whitish below.
- The flowers are small and greenish.
- The fruit is a glossy, egg-shaped berry.

The tiny male flowers are greenish-yellow.

**FACT FILE**

**Region of origin**
Eastern North America.
**Height** 25m/82ft
**Shape** Broadly columnar
**Deciduous**
**Pollinated** Insect
**Leaf shape** Obovate

# Common Hazel

*Corylus avellana*

There is much discussion as to whether the hazel is a tree or a shrub. In theory, a tree should have 1m/3ft of clear stem before it branches or forks, and it should be able to grow to 6m/20ft. The common hazel can certainly grow that tall, but it often forks low down. This forking habit is encouraged by the fact that for centuries, right across Europe, hazel has regularly been coppiced (cut down) to ground level in order to make it grow more thickly. The fact that it regrows even after a harsh pruning makes it popular for field hedges.

▲ *The deep green leaves turn yellow then brown in autumn.*

*This tree produces the popular hazelnut.*

## IDENTIFICATION

- The bark is smooth and silvery-grey to pale brown.

- The buds are small, brown and ovoid. Like the leave and shoots, they have thick hairs on them.

- The leaves are up to 10cm/4in across with double teeth around the edge. They are thick and rough.

- The male flowers are yellow catkins and the females are tiny red flowers. Both grow on the same shoot.

- The fruit is a round to ovoid, light brown-coloured edible nut, half encased in a green calyx.

*The tiny red female flowers grow on plump green buds.*

*The male catkins release large amounts of pollen in early spring.*

## FACT FILE

**Region of origin**
Europe into western Asia and North Africa.
**Height** 15m/50ft
**Shape** Broadly spreading
**Deciduous**
**Pollinated** Wind
**Leaf shape** Orbicular

# Paperbark Maple

*Acer griseum*

This beautiful small tree was discovered in 1901 and almost immediately became a garden favourite. Its most distinguishing feature is its striking, cinnamon-coloured, wafer-thin bark, which peels away in strips to reveal fresh orange bark underneath. It also has attractive autumn leaf colour and winged seeds.

## IDENTIFICATION

- The bark is reddish-brown and flaking.
- The buds are pointed and very dark brown.
- The leaves are up to 10cm/4in long, with several large blunt teeth on each side.
- The flowers are greenish-yellow on stalks.
- The fruits are pairs of winged seeds.

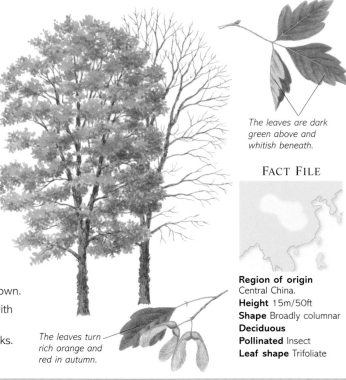

The leaves are dark green above and whitish beneath.

The leaves turn rich orange and red in autumn.

### FACT FILE

**Region of origin** Central China.
**Height** 15m/50ft
**Shape** Broadly columnar
**Deciduous**
**Pollinated** Insect
**Leaf shape** Trifoliate

---

# Smooth Japanese Maple

*Acer palmatum*

Hundreds of different varieties of the smooth Japanese maple are grown in Europe. This tree species is grown for its spreading shape, which is like a large natural bonsai, and its finely toothed leaves, which have lovely autumn colour.

## IDENTIFICATION

- The bark is grey-brown and smooth.
- The ovoid buds are reddish-green.
- The purplish-red flowers grow in clusters.
- The leaves are 10cm/4in long, with five to seven lobes and forward-facing teeth.
- The fruits are pairs of winged seeds.

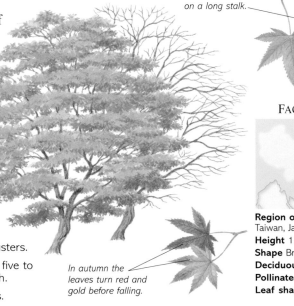

The green to red winged seeds grow in clusters of pairs on a long stalk.

In autumn the leaves turn red and gold before falling.

### FACT FILE

**Region of origin** China, Taiwan, Japan and Korea.
**Height** 15m/50ft
**Shape** Broadly spreading
**Deciduous**
**Pollinated** Insect
**Leaf shape** Palmate

# Norway Maple

*Acer platanoides*

This fast-growing, handsome, hardy maple has been cultivated as an ornamental species for centuries. It has a large spreading crown with branches that grow upwards. It is as much at home in parkland settings as in woodland. The distinguishing features of this tree are its superb autumn leaf colours (they change from bright green to gold, orange-brown and red in a splendid display) and its bright yellow flowers, which emerge just before the leaves appear.

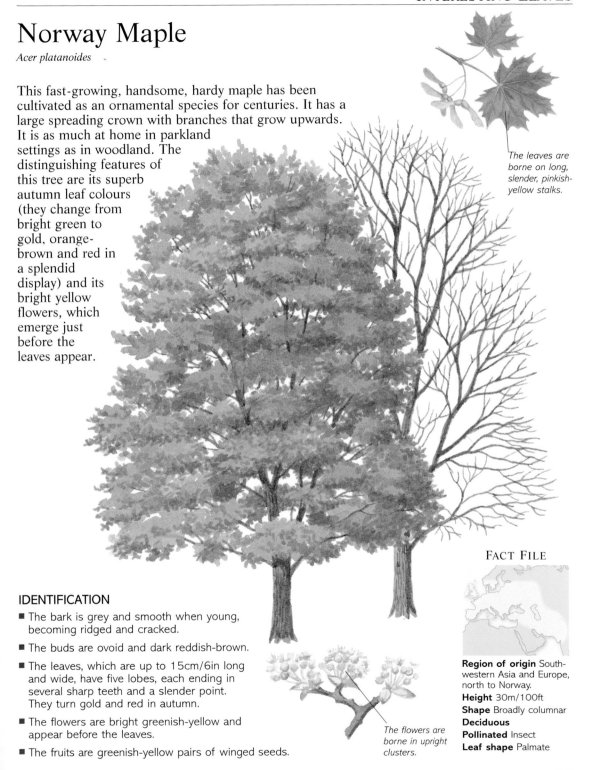

The leaves are borne on long, slender, pinkish-yellow stalks.

## IDENTIFICATION

- The bark is grey and smooth when young, becoming ridged and cracked.

- The buds are ovoid and dark reddish-brown.

- The leaves, which are up to 15cm/6in long and wide, have five lobes, each ending in several sharp teeth and a slender point. They turn gold and red in autumn.

- The flowers are bright greenish-yellow and appear before the leaves.

- The fruits are greenish-yellow pairs of winged seeds.

The flowers are borne in upright clusters.

## FACT FILE

**Region of origin** South-western Asia and Europe, north to Norway.
**Height** 30m/100ft
**Shape** Broadly columnar
**Deciduous**
**Pollinated** Insect
**Leaf shape** Palmate

59

# Silver Maple

*Acer saccharinum*

This is one of the fastest-growing North American maples and is widely planted as an attractive tree in parks and gardens. It has a light, open top, with two-coloured leaves (borne on stalks up to 15cm/6in long), which catch the light as they flutter in the breeze. It does have rather brittle wood, which means that it has a tendency to drop its branches – sometimes with no warning.

*The leaves are mid-green above and much paler below.*

*The trunk often has shoots and suckers growing out of it.*

## IDENTIFICATION

- The bark is smooth and grey when young, becoming flaky.

- The leaves are up to 15cm/6in long and wide and have five sharply toothed lobes, each ending in a sharp point.

- The male and female flowers are small and greenish-yellow and clustered on the young shoots as the leaves emerge.

- The fruits are winged seeds carried in pairs.

*In mid-autumn the leaves turn yellow-brown before falling.*

## FACT FILE

**Region of origin**
Europe eastwards to northern Iran and the Atlas mountains of North Africa.
**Height** 20m/65ft
**Shape** Broadly conical
**Deciduous**
**Pollinated** Wind
**Leaf shape** Linear

# Lombardy Poplar

*Populus nigra* 'Italica'

The Lombardy poplar is probably one of the most easily recognizable of all trees because of its slender, column-like outline and very upright branches, which grow almost from ground level, leaving a very short trunk. It is a variety of the black poplar, *Populus nigra*, and is widely planted for shade and as an ornamental tree. Lombardy poplars are nearly all male trees, so new trees have to be grown from cuttings rather than seeds.

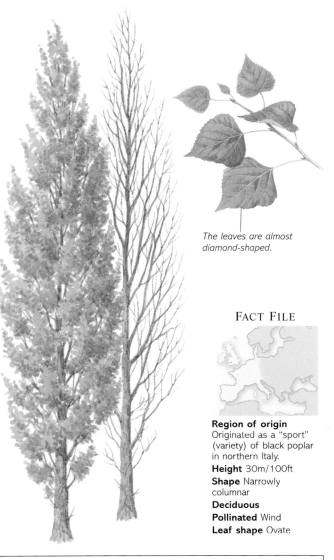

*The leaves are almost diamond-shaped.*

*Male catkins are red and full of pollen.*

## IDENTIFICATION

- The bark is dark grey and grooved.
- The buds are ovoid, pale brown and pointed.
- The leaves are triangular- to diamond-shaped, bright glossy green and up to 10cm/4in wide.
- The male catkins are up to 7.5cm/3in long, grey turning crimson; the females are greenish, later turning white with seed.

## FACT FILE

**Region of origin**
Originated as a "sport" (variety) of black poplar in northern Italy.
**Height** 30m/100ft
**Shape** Narrowly columnar
**Deciduous**
**Pollinated** Wind
**Leaf shape** Ovate

# White Poplar

*Populus alba*

This tree, which is native to Europe, western Asia and parts of North Africa, is often planted alongside motorways, where it is able to cope with the atmospheric pollution. It has a stout trunk, which is seldom upright, and branches that twist as they grow. The bark is light greyish-green and smooth when young, but darkens and roughens with age. The leaves have three to five lobes and are up to 6cm/2⅓in wide. They are dark greyish-green above and have silvery-white undersides. Like the silver maple and the whitebeam, the white poplar looks stunning when the leaves blow in the wind to reveal their two colours. The flowers are catkins, which appear before the leaves: the males are grey with crimson stamens and the females are green.

# Aspen

European aspen *Populus tremula*

The botanical name for this species, *tremula*, comes from the fact that the leaves, which are borne on slender, flattened leaf stalks, tremble and quiver in even the slightest breeze. The aspen is a medium-sized tree, growing to 20m/66ft, with branches that grow upwards. The leaves are 7.5cm/3in long and wide. They emerge a pink-bronze colour from the bud in spring, gradually turning a dull rich green by early summer, with paler undersides. The catkins emerge before the leaves.

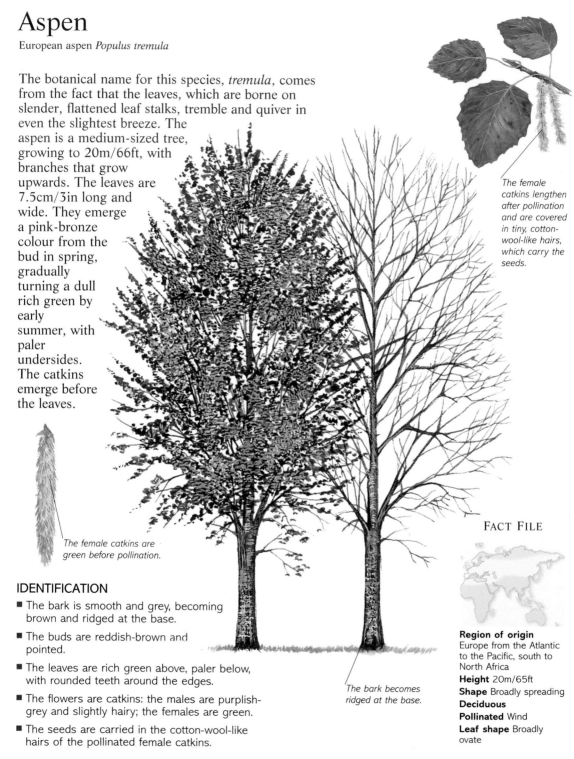

The female catkins lengthen after pollination and are covered in tiny, cotton-wool-like hairs, which carry the seeds.

The female catkins are green before pollination.

## IDENTIFICATION

- The bark is smooth and grey, becoming brown and ridged at the base.

- The buds are reddish-brown and pointed.

- The leaves are rich green above, paler below, with rounded teeth around the edges.

- The flowers are catkins: the males are purplish-grey and slightly hairy; the females are green.

- The seeds are carried in the cotton-wool-like hairs of the pollinated female catkins.

The bark becomes ridged at the base.

## FACT FILE

**Region of origin**
Europe from the Atlantic to the Pacific, south to North Africa
**Height** 20m/65ft
**Shape** Broadly spreading
**Deciduous**
**Pollinated** Wind
**Leaf shape** Broadly ovate

# Western Balsam Poplar

Black cottonwood *Populus trichocarpa*

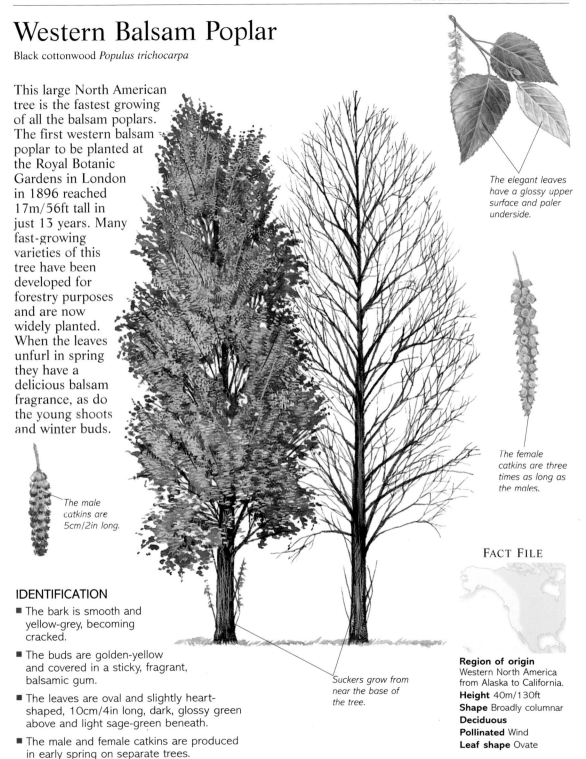

This large North American tree is the fastest growing of all the balsam poplars. The first western balsam poplar to be planted at the Royal Botanic Gardens in London in 1896 reached 17m/56ft tall in just 13 years. Many fast-growing varieties of this tree have been developed for forestry purposes and are now widely planted. When the leaves unfurl in spring they have a delicious balsam fragrance, as do the young shoots and winter buds.

The elegant leaves have a glossy upper surface and paler underside.

The female catkins are three times as long as the males.

The male catkins are 5cm/2in long.

## IDENTIFICATION

- The bark is smooth and yellow-grey, becoming cracked.

- The buds are golden-yellow and covered in a sticky, fragrant, balsamic gum.

- The leaves are oval and slightly heart-shaped, 10cm/4in long, dark, glossy green above and light sage-green beneath.

- The male and female catkins are produced in early spring on separate trees.

Suckers grow from near the base of the tree.

## FACT FILE

**Region of origin**
Western North America from Alaska to California.
**Height** 40m/130ft
**Shape** Broadly columnar
**Deciduous**
**Pollinated** Wind
**Leaf shape** Ovate

# Flowers and Fruit

Like the flowers in a garden, the flowers on trees vary enormously in shape, colour, scent, complexity of formation and grouping on the twig. From the tiny, rounded, fragrant yellow flowers of the mimosa to the massive, showy white blooms of the bull bay, a tree's flowers can be stunning in many different ways. As for the fruit, this comes in a wide variety of forms, including fleshy fruits such as apples and pears, berries such as holly, nuts such as acorns and walnuts, seed pods such as laburnum, and winged seeds like sycamore.

## Tulip Tree

Yellow poplar *Liriodendron tulipifera*

This magnificent tree stands out from the crowd for several reasons, including its size, its flowers, its leaf shape and its adaptability – it can grow in severe Canadian winters and sub-tropical Florida summers. The tulip tree's unusual flowers are produced in summer once the tree reaches 12–15 years old. They are tulip-shaped, have six petals and three sepals and are a mixture of green and yellowy-orange.

### IDENTIFICATION

- The bark is grey-brown and smooth, becoming cracked.
- The buds are a glossy reddish-brown with curved tips.
- The leaves are dark green and lobed on each side, with a cut-off indented tip. The underside is almost bluish-white.
- The flowers are 6cm/2½in long and tulip-shaped, containing a bright cluster of orange-yellow stamens.

*Adult tulip trees have clear, straight trunks and broad tops.*

The leaves ▶ and flowers change colour at the same time of year.

In autumn, the leaves turn orange-yellow before falling.

FACT FILE

**Region of origin**
Eastern North America from Ontario to New York in the north, and to Florida in the south.
**Height** 50m/165ft
**Shape** Broadly columnar
**Deciduous**
**Pollinated** Bee
**Leaf shape** Palmate

# Handkerchief Tree

Dove tree, Ghost tree *Davidia involucrata*

This beautiful tree was first introduced into the West from China in 1904. All of its common names refer to the white hanging leaf bracts that appear in late spring. These bracts, which appear in pairs and are of unequal size, flutter in the breeze, creating a stunning effect as they contrast with the bright green leaves. They surround the sweetly scented flowers, which are tiny, with lilac-coloured anthers and no petals, and their role is to attract moths to the flowers in order to pollinate them.

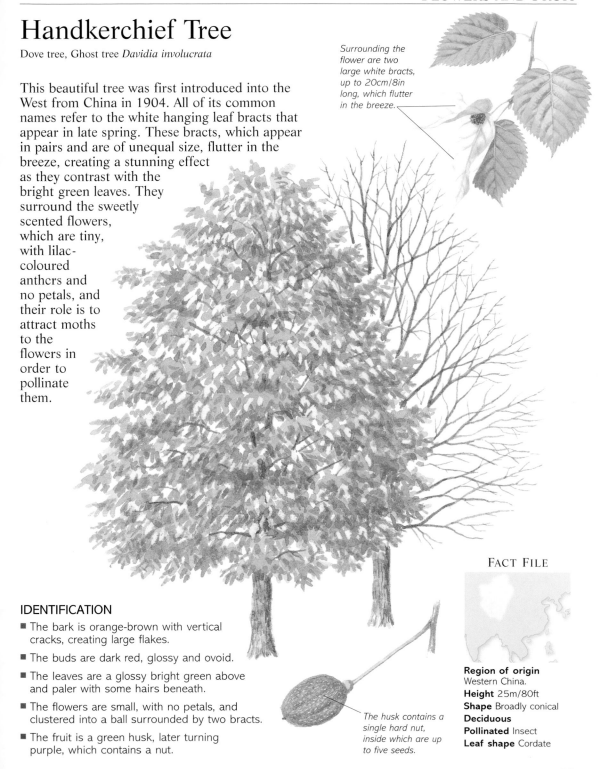

Surrounding the flower are two large white bracts, up to 20cm/8in long, which flutter in the breeze.

## IDENTIFICATION

- The bark is orange-brown with vertical cracks, creating large flakes.

- The buds are dark red, glossy and ovoid.

- The leaves are a glossy bright green above and paler with some hairs beneath.

- The flowers are small, with no petals, and clustered into a ball surrounded by two bracts.

- The fruit is a green husk, later turning purple, which contains a nut.

The husk contains a single hard nut, inside which are up to five seeds.

## FACT FILE

**Region of origin** Western China.
**Height** 25m/80ft
**Shape** Broadly conical
**Deciduous**
**Pollinated** Insect
**Leaf shape** Cordate

# Plum

*Prunus domestica*

The origins of the garden plum tree are lost in the mists of time. It is probably a hybrid, possibly between the sloe, *Prunus spinosa*, and the cherry plum, *Prunus cerasifera*. In the future, DNA examination may be able to unravel the mystery. There are countless different types of plum, all developed to make the delicious fruit taste even better. If it did not have any fruit, this tree would probably not be widely grown.

*The flowers are slightly fragrant.*

▲ *The plum fruit can be green, yellow, red or purple.*

*Plums come in many different colours but are always ovoid.*

## IDENTIFICATION

- The bark is brown-grey.

- The buds are small, brown and covered in fine hair.

- The leaves are up to 7.5cm/3in long, dull grass-green and have blunt teeth.

- The flowers are white, about 2.5cm/1in across and borne in spring before the leaves appear.

- The fruits are succulent drupes with a single seed or stone (pit).

*The bark develops cracks as the tree gets older.*

### FACT FILE

**Region of origin**
Unknown but probably a hybrid of garden origin.
**Height** 10m/30ft
**Shape** Broadly spreading
**Deciduous**
**Pollinated** Insect
**Leaf shape** Elliptic to obovate

# Sargent's Cherry

*Prunus sargentii*

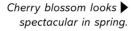
Cherry blossom looks ▶ spectacular in spring.

This fast-growing tree is one of the loveliest of all the cherries, producing a mass of rich pink, single flowers coupled with bronze-coloured young leaves in spring and brilliant orange-red leaf colours in autumn.

## IDENTIFICATION

- The bark is a deep brownish-red.
- The buds are dark red and pointed.
- The leaves are a deep grass-green.
- The flowers are a rich pink colour.
- The fruit is a blackish ovoid drupe.

The flowers are pink.

### FACT FILE

**Region of origin** Northern Japan, Korea and the island of Sakhalin.
**Height** 20m/65ft
**Shape** Broadly spreading
**Deciduous**
**Pollinated** Insect
**Leaf shape** Elliptic to obovate

# Tibetan Cherry

*Prunus serrula*

The cherries are egg-shaped.

The Tibetan cherry tree has beautiful bark, which is like highly polished, deep-red mahogany, marked into sections by light brown horizontal bands. The leaves, which are also attractive, are willow-like, with fine teeth and a long pointed tip. The flowers are white.

## IDENTIFICATION

- The bark is shiny red.
- The buds are ovoid, chestnut-brown.
- The leaves are mid-green and pointed.
- The flowers are 2cm/¾in across and white.
- The fruit is crimson and ovoid, borne in pairs.

### FACT FILE

**Region of origin** Western China.
**Height** 15m/50ft
**Shape** Broadly spreading
**Deciduous**
**Pollinated** Insect
**Leaf shape** Lanceolate

# Medlar

*Mespilus germanica*

This small, spreading tree has rather tangled branches. It is grown mainly for its fruit, which needs to have started rotting before it is edible. The flowers, up to 5cm/2in across, appear in early summer. The fruits have a tasselled look.

The flowers open in summer.

## IDENTIFICATION

- The bark is dull brown, developing cracks.
- The buds are green-brown and hairy.
- The leaves are bright green and lightly toothed.
- The flowers are white with five petals.
- The fruit is russet-brown and 3cm/1¼in across.

The fruit is like a flattened pear in shape, with a slightly open brown top.

### FACT FILE

**Region of origin** South-western Asia and south-eastern Europe.
**Height** 6m/20ft
**Shape** Broadly spreading
**Deciduous**
**Pollinated** Insect
**Leaf shape** Elliptic to lanceolate

---

# Quince

*Cydonia oblonga*

Like many trees long cultivated for their fruit, the exact origins of the common quince are not known. It has certainly been grown around the Mediterranean for at least 1,000 years. The bark, which is smooth at first, flakes to reveal orange-brown fresh bark beneath. The leaves are up to 10cm/4in long and have brownish-grey hairs on the underside.

Quince fruit is fragrant and bitter.

The leaves are smooth and stay on the tree until the winter.

## IDENTIFICATION

- The bark is brownish-purple.
- The buds are ovoid.
- The leaves are dark green.
- The flowers are white, flushed with pink.
- The fruits are golden-yellow, pear-shaped and quite waxy.

### FACT FILE

**Region of origin** South-western Asia.
**Height** 5m/16ft
**Shape** Broadly spreading
**Deciduous**
**Pollinated** Insect
**Leaf shape** Ovate to elliptic

# Crab Apple

*Malus sylvestris*

This tree is known to many as the "sour little apple", for its great quantities of small green apples, inedible unless made into jelly. The wild crab apple is one of the parents of the domestic orchard apple, *Malus domestica*.

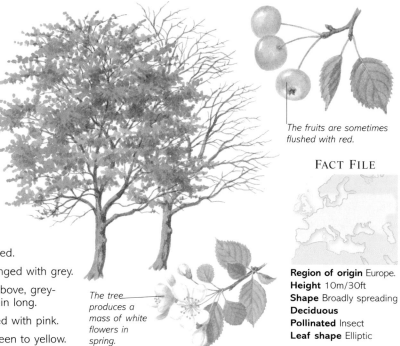

The fruits are sometimes flushed with red.

## IDENTIFICATION

- The bark is brown and cracked.
- The buds are dark purple fringed with grey.
- The leaves are deep green above, grey-green beneath, and 4cm/1½in long.
- The flowers are white, flushed with pink.
- The fruit is apple-like and green to yellow.

The tree produces a mass of white flowers in spring.

### FACT FILE

**Region of origin** Europe.
**Height** 10m/30ft
**Shape** Broadly spreading
**Deciduous**
**Pollinated** Insect
**Leaf shape** Elliptic

---

# Siberian Crab

*Malus baccata*

This small to medium-sized tree has a rounded shape when young, becoming spreading with age. The species name *baccata* means a fruit with a fleshy coat. In Siberia, the fruits are made into wine and jelly. The tree's bark flakes to reveal fresh reddish-brown bark beneath. The leaves are up to 7.5cm/3in long.

The leaves have very fine teeth around the edges.

The fruit starts out yellow and slowly turns red.

## IDENTIFICATION

- The bark is brown.
- The buds are purple-brown.
- The leaves are dark green above, paler beneath.
- The flowers are white flushed with pink and borne in clusters.
- The fruit is a small, rounded "apple".

### FACT FILE

**Region of origin**
Eastern Siberia, Mongolia, northern China and Korea.
**Height** 15m/50ft
**Shape** Broadly spreading
**Deciduous**
**Pollinated** Insect
**Leaf shape** Ovate to elliptic

# Hybrid Strawberry Tree

*Arbutus* x *andrachnoides*

Hanging clusters of ▶
*flowers appear on the tree
from autumn to spring.*

This natural hybrid between the
Irish and Grecian strawberry
trees occurs in Greece, where
both parents grow wild. It
is widely planted for its
attractive leaves, which
have a bright yellow midrib,
and its bark, which peels
from the trunk in long strips
to reveal paler new bark.

*The fruits,
which ripen
from green
to orange-
red, contain
countless
seeds.*

### IDENTIFICATION

- The bark is a cinnamon-
brown colour.

- The leaves are 10cm/4in long,
thick and rigid, shiny dark green above
and whitish beneath.

- The flowers are small, white and urn-shaped.

- The fruits are produced only rarely.

*The flowers
are slightly
fragrant.*

## FACT FILE

**Region of origin** Greece.
**Height** 10m/30ft
**Shape** Broadly spreading
**Evergreen**
**Pollinated** Insect
**Leaf shape** Ovate to
elliptic

---

# Hawthorn

May *Crataegus monogyna*

*The fruits are a
shiny dark red.*

This is a slow-growing, hardy tree, which
has been used for centuries to both
shelter animals and enclose
them. With its sharp thorns,
a well-clipped hawthorn
hedge is a very effective
windbreak and barrier. Its
name "may" refers to the
month when it is covered
with white flowers.

▲ *A profusion of
creamy white flowers
appear in spring.*

## FACT FILE

### IDENTIFICATION

- The bark is dull brown.

- The leaves are leathery,
dark green above and paler,
with some tufts of hair, beneath.

- The flowers are creamy-white and scented.

- The fruits are ovoid red berries.

*The twigs
have vicious
thorns.*

**Region of origin** Europe.
**Height** 10m/30ft
**Shape** Broadly spreading
**Deciduous**
**Pollinated** Insect
**Leaf shape** Obovate

# Foxglove Tree

*Paulownia tomentosa*

This beautiful flowering tree comes from the mountains of central China. Its pale purple, foxglove-like flowers appear on upright spikes in late spring. The leaves are massive – measuring up to 45cm/18in long and wide – and hairy.

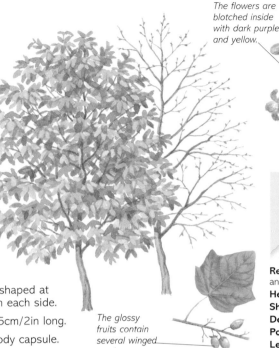

The flowers are blotched inside with dark purple and yellow.

## IDENTIFICATION

- The bark is grey and smooth.
- The dark green leaves are heart-shaped at the base, with two large lobes on each side.
- The flowers are pale purple and 5cm/2in long.
- The fruit is a green, pointed, woody capsule.

The glossy fruits contain several winged seeds.

### FACT FILE

**Region of origin** Central and eastern China.
**Height** 20m/65ft
**Shape** Broadly columnar
**Deciduous**
**Pollinated** Insect
**Leaf shape** Ovate

# Osage Orange

*Maclura pomifera*

This tree is best known for its showy, orange-like fruits, which are actually clusters of smaller fruits that have fused together. The fruit is inedible, and, when fresh, full of a sour milky juice. The branches of the Osage orange are often twisted.

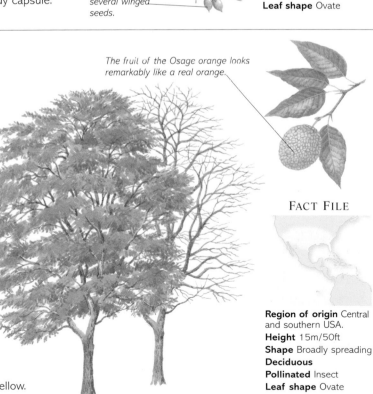

The fruit of the Osage orange looks remarkably like a real orange.

## IDENTIFICATION

- The bark is orange-brown.
- The leaves are a glossy rich green above and paler below, 10cm/4in long and pointed.
- Male and female flowers are yellow-green and produced on separate trees.
- The fruits are green, ripening to yellow.

### FACT FILE

**Region of origin** Central and southern USA.
**Height** 15m/50ft
**Shape** Broadly spreading
**Deciduous**
**Pollinated** Insect
**Leaf shape** Ovate

# Common Laburnum

*Laburnum anagyroides*

This beautiful tree grows in mountainous areas of central Europe at heights of up to 2,000m/6,500ft. It is a small, spreading, short-lived tree, which is best known for its masses of hanging, golden yellow flowers. It is widely grown in Europe in parks and gardens. All parts of the tree contain a substance that is poisonous if eaten. The green, unripe seed pods are particularly dangerous.

The seed pods ripen from green to brown.

▲ The bright yellow flowers appear in late spring.

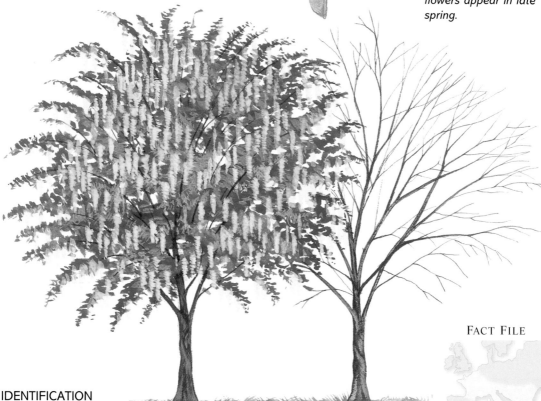

## IDENTIFICATION

- The bark is dark brown-grey and smooth, becoming lightly cracked as it ages.

- The buds are covered with silver hairs.

- The leaves are up to 10cm/4in long, rich green above, grey-green beneath and covered with silver hairs when young.

- The flowers are golden-yellow and hang in sprays of up to 30cm/12in long.

- The fruits are hairy seed pods.

Laburnum leaves grow in threes.

## FACT FILE

**Region of origin**
Central and southern Europe from France to Hungary and Bulgaria.

**Height** 9m/30ft

**Shape** Broadly spreading

**Deciduous**

**Pollinated** Insect

**Leaf shape** Trifoliate

# Bull Bay Magnolia

*Magnolia grandiflora*

This magnificent evergreen flowering tree is usually grown against a wall in cooler regions to protect it from excess cold and frost in winter. In a warm, sheltered, sunny garden, however, it will grow into a spreading, short-stemmed tree. The bull bay grows best near the coast and on ground no higher than 150m/500ft. The combination of glossy, dark green, leathery leaves and creamy white flowers, which have a delicious scent, makes it a very popular garden tree. It has flowers on it from summer right through to late autumn, and the large pale flowers make a striking contrast with the dark leaves.

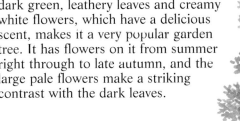

The leaf backs are copper-coloured.

The red seed pods appear from midsummer.

The spectacular flowers are like dinner plates, measuring up to 30cm/12in across.

## IDENTIFICATION

- The bark is grey-brown, cracking into plates.

- The oval leaves grow up to 25cm/10in long, are dark green above and either pale green or covered in copper-coloured hairs beneath.

- The flowers are wide-brimmed and cup-shaped, creamy white to pale lemon, but will not appear on the tree until it is at least 10 years old.

- The fruits cluster together into reddish seed pods carried on thick stalks.

### FACT FILE

**Region of origin** North American south-eastern coastal strip from North Carolina to Florida and west along the Gulf to south-eastern Texas.
**Height** 25m/82ft
**Shape** Broadly conical
**Evergreen**
**Pollinated** Insect
**Leaf shape** Elliptic to ovate

# Star Magnolia

*Magnolia stellata*

This slow-growing, small Japanese tree, or large shrub, seldom reaches more than 3m/10ft tall. It flowers on bare branches in late winter and early spring, and this early flowering means that it can be damaged by frosts. The flowers are pure white at first, later turning pale pink and star-shaped. They have 12–18 petals and are scented.

# Mimosa

*Silver wattle Acacia dealbata*

This tree is extremely popular for planting as an ornamental street tree in Mediterranean countries, but does not grow as well in the more northerly parts of Europe. It is prized by florists for its delicate, feathery leaves and fragrant yellow flowers.

## IDENTIFICATION

- The bark is grey-green when young, later turning grey and grooved.
- The leaves are up to 12cm/4¾in long and have countless small, blue-green, hairy leaflets.
- The flowers are small and rounded, sulphur-yellow and fragrant.
- The fruits are flat, bluish-white seed pods, ripening to brown.

*The scented flowers appear from late winter into early spring.*

*The flat seed pod is up to 7.5cm/3in long.*

### FACT FILE

**Region of origin**
South-eastern Australia and Tasmania.
**Height** 25m/80ft
**Shape** Broadly conical
**Evergreen**
**Pollinated** Insect
**Leaf shape** Bipinnate

---

# Indian Bean Tree

*Catalpa bignonioides*

The Indian referred to in the name is the Native American, who used to dry and paint catalpa seeds and wear them as decoration. The tree has a spreading shape and is often planted in towns and cities. The leaves emerge from the bud bronze-coloured, gradually turning grass-green.

*The flowers are ▶ trumpet-shaped and spotted with yellow and purple.*

*The long, thin seed pods stay on the tree all winter.*

## IDENTIFICATION

- The bark is grey-brown.
- The buds are tiny and orange-brown.
- The leaves are up to 25cm/10in long.
- The flowers are white with frilled edges.
- The fruits are slender brown seed pods.

### FACT FILE

**Region of origin**
Southern-east USA.
**Height** 20m/65ft
**Shape** Broadly spreading
**Deciduous**
**Pollinated** Insect
**Leaf shape** Ovate

# Pagoda Tree

*Sophora japonica*

Despite its species name, *japonica*, the pagoda tree is thought not to come from Japan. However, it has been widely grown there for centuries, particularly in temple gardens and places of learning. In China, the flower buds were used to make a yellow dye. The overall shape of the tree is rounded, with branches starting low on the trunk. Flowers on trees grown from seed take anything up to 30 years to appear.

*The creamy white flowers are shaped like those of the sweet pea.*

## IDENTIFICATION

- The bark is greenish-brown.
- The buds are small and scaly.
- The leaves are up to 25cm/10in long, with up to 15 pointed leaflets growing opposite each other, dark green above and whitish below.
- The flowers are white, pea-like, fragrant and borne in hanging clusters in summer.
- The fruits are brown seed pods up to 7.5cm/3in long, containing up to six seeds.

*The bark becomes cracked and ridged as the tree gets older.*

## FACT FILE

**Region of origin**
Northern China but could be more widespread.
**Height** 20m/65ft
**Shape** Broadly spreading
**Deciduous**
**Pollinated** Insect
**Leaf shape** Pinnate

# Common Walnut

*Juglans regia*

Although the walnut tree is naturally widespread, it has also been cultivated for its nuts since Roman times, when it was introduced to Britain. The male and female flowers are both yellowish-green catkins, though the males are reddish at first and grow singly. The females develop into drupes containing the walnuts.

*Walnuts are ▶ protected by a smooth shell.*

*Male catkins turn yellowish-green before falling.*

## IDENTIFICATION

- The bark is pale grey with black cracks.
- The buds are purple-brown.
- The leaves are a deep, dull green.
- The flowers are greenish catkins.
- The fruits are brown walnuts.

*Inside each husk is a walnut.*

### FACT FILE

**Region of origin**
From Greece in the west to central China and Japan in the east.
**Height** 30m/100ft
**Shape** Broadly spreading
**Deciduous**
**Pollinated** Wind
**Leaf shape** Pinnate

# Mulberry

*Morus nigra*

This is the black mulberry, rather than the Chinese white mulberry, *Morus alba*, which is the one on which silkworms flourish. It does, however, produce lovely sweet fruit in late summer. The tree is low-growing, with a wide domed top.

*A mulberry fruit ripens from green to red to dark purple, when it is sweet to eat.*

## IDENTIFICATION

- The bark is orange.
- The buds are purple-brown and shiny.
- The leaves are bright green, heart-shaped, and have small teeth.
- The flowers are cone-like structures.
- The fruit is raspberry-like.

*Mulberry trunks become gnarled and often start to lean, or even fall over, at a young age.*

### FACT FILE

**Region of origin**
Western Asia.
**Height** 10m/30ft
**Shape** Broadly spreading
**Deciduous**
**Pollinated** Insect
**Leaf shape** Ovate

76

# Caucasian Wing Nut

*Pterocarya fraxinifolia*

The natural habitat of the Caucasian wing nut is damp woodland next to rivers and marshland. It is a very fast-growing species, quite regularly achieving 3m/10ft of growth in one year. The winter buds are naked, with brown, hairy bud leaves. The leaves are up to 60cm/ 24in long and made up of 23 slightly toothed dark green leaflets, each up to 15cm/6in long. The flowers are carried in hanging catkins.

The nut-like fruit has a pair of semi-circular wings.

The nuts are borne in hanging "necklaces" up to 50cm/20in long.

## IDENTIFICATION

- The bark is light grey, smooth when young, turning deeply cracked later.

- The buds are dark brown and hairy.

- The leaves are a glossy dark green above and paler below.

- The flowers are small and green and carried in hanging catkins in spring.

- The fruits are wing nuts: winged fruits that turn brown when ripe.

◀ *Female*     *Male* ▶

*The male catkin is much shorter than the female, which is shown here in flower, with its red-tipped stigmas.*

## FACT FILE

**Region of origin** From the Caucasus Mountains in Russia, the eastern shore of the Black Sea, southern shore of the Caspian Sea and into the north of Iran.
**Height** 30m/100ft
**Shape** Broadly spreading
**Deciduous**
**Pollinated** Wind
**Leaf shape** Pinnate

77

# Japanese Snowbell Tree

*Styrax japonica*

This beautiful, small, spreading tree, which was first brought from Japan to the West in 1862, ought to be much better known and more widely planted than it is. It is ideal for a small garden, as it seldom reaches more than 7m/25ft tall, and is happy growing even in cooler regions. The tree has a rounded shape, with long, arching branches, so that it is often wider than it is tall. The leaves are bay-like, tapering to a point at both ends, and up to 10cm/4in long. The open bell-shaped flowers are borne in clusters all along the branches in early summer.

*The leaves are like those of the bay laurel and usually grow in groups of three.*

*The bell-shaped flowers have yellow anthers.*

## IDENTIFICATION

- The bark is orange-brown, smooth at first, later becoming cracked.

- The buds are small and pale clear brown.

- The leaves are a rich shiny green above, paler green beneath and have small, shallow teeth.

- The flowers are creamy-white, slightly fragrant and hang in small clusters on long stalks.

- The fruits are ovoid greenish berries containing a single seed.

*Once pollinated, the hanging flowers form green-grey berries in a bright green, purple-tipped cup.*

FACT FILE

**Region of origin** Japan, Korea and China.
**Height** 10m/30ft
**Shape** Broadly spreading
**Deciduous**
**Pollinated** Insect
**Leaf shape** Oval to elliptic

# Common Holly

*Ilex aquifolium*

Holly is one of the most useful and attractive trees in Europe. It is extremely hardy, and its thick leaves provide better shelter in unprotected coastal and mountain areas than just about any other tree. Holly has long been considered an important part of Christmas celebrations, and its bright berries cheer up the dullest winter days. Holly timber is dense and hard and has been used for making just about everything, from piano keys to billiard cues. The leaves are extremely variable: some leaves have strong spines around the edges, while others are spineless. They also vary in colouring: some have silver or gold on them.

▲ *The thickly growing leaves make holly a useful hedging plant.*

*The red berries, which are borne in clusters along the shoot in winter, are poisonous.*

## IDENTIFICATION

- The bark is silver-grey and smooth, becoming rougher with age.

- The leaves are up to 10cm/4in long, glossy dark green and waxy above, and pale green beneath.

- Male and female flowers are small and white with a slight fragrance; they are borne on separate trees in late spring and early summer.

- The fruits are round, shiny, bright red berries.

*Holly flowers are scented and appear from spring to summer.*

## FACT FILE

**Region of origin** Whole of Europe, western Asia and North Africa.
**Height** 20m/65ft
**Shape** Broadly columnar
**Evergreen**
**Pollinated** Insect
**Leaf shape** Elliptic to ovate

79

# Amazing Trees

The broadleaf trees of Europe include some of the most familiar of all trees, whether growing in towns, parks or woodland. The most well-known are included here, and you should be able to visit all of them in local parkland or out in the countryside near your home. These trees are widely regarded with affection and include the majestic oak, with its autumn acorns; tall, spreading horse chestnuts, with their "candles" of flowers and spiky clusters of nuts; silver birches, with their beautiful bark and bright green leaves; and ash trees, with their "keys".

## Silver Birch

*Betula pendula*

The silver birch is one of the toughest of all trees, able to survive intense cold and long periods of drought. Birch was one of the first trees to colonize northern Europe after the last ice age 12,000 years ago. It has a light-coloured bark, with dark markings developing on older trees. The leaves are 6cm/2½in across and turn butter-yellow in autumn. Skis were made from the hard, strong wood.

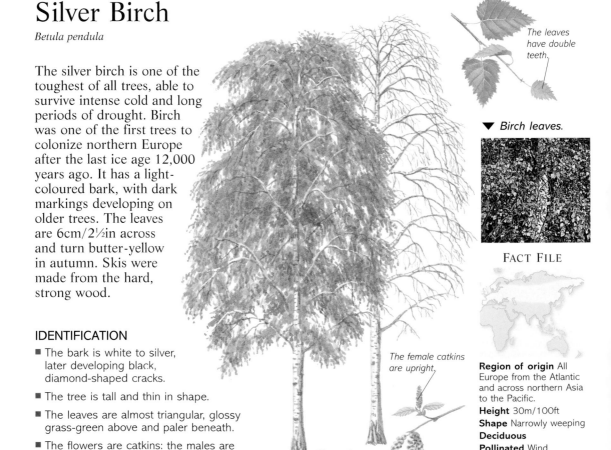

The leaves have double teeth.

▼ Birch leaves.

FACT FILE

The female catkins are upright.

The male catkins hang down.

### IDENTIFICATION

- The bark is white to silver, later developing black, diamond-shaped cracks.
- The tree is tall and thin in shape.
- The leaves are almost triangular, glossy grass-green above and paler beneath.
- The flowers are catkins: the males are brownish-yellow and the females are green.
- The fruits are small winged seeds.

**Region of origin** All Europe from the Atlantic and across northern Asia to the Pacific.
**Height** 30m/100ft
**Shape** Narrowly weeping
**Deciduous**
**Pollinated** Wind
**Leaf shape** Ovate to triangular

80

# Oriental Plane

*Platanus orientalis*

The Oriental plane is one of the largest and longest-lived of all the deciduous trees that grow in temperate climates. It can reach heights of over 30m/100ft, with a trunk that measures 6m/20ft around. The leaves are wider than they are long, and cut into five narrow lobes. In autumn they turn yellow, then gold and finally bronze.

The fruit stays on the tree all winter.

▼ *Oriental plane leaf.*

## IDENTIFICATION

- The bark is buff-grey.
- The buds are red-brown.
- The leaves are shiny green above, paler below.
- The flower balls are yellowish (male) and dark red (female), on long stalks.
- The brown, ball-like fruits grow in clusters.

The trunk is often crooked.

### FACT FILE

**Region of origin**
Greece, Albania, Cyprus, Lebanon, Syria and Israel.
**Height** 30m/100ft
**Shape** Broadly spreading
**Deciduous**
**Pollinated** Insect
**Leaf shape** Palmate lobed

# London Plane

*Platanus* x *hispanica*

This tree is widely planted in cities across the world because of its ability to survive atmospheric pollution and hard pruning. It grows up to 35m/115ft tall, with wide-spreading branches. The bark flakes off to reveal paler patches below, creating a mottled pattern. The five-lobed leaves look like maples.

▼ *London plane leaf.*

## IDENTIFICATION

- The bark is grey-brown and smooth.
- The buds are red-brown with curved tips.
- The leaves are shiny green above, paler below.
- The flower balls are yellowish (male) and dark red (female), on long stalks.
- The brown, ball-like fruits grow in clusters.

### FACT FILE

**Region of origin**
South-eastern Europe and North America.
**Height** 22m/70ft
**Shape** Spreading
**Deciduous**
**Pollinated** Insect
**Leaf shape** Palmate lobed

# Wych Elm

*Ulmus glabra*

The flowers have dark red anthers.

This tough, medium-sized tree survives particularly well in unprotected coastal areas and on mountain slopes. It has strong, solid timber, which is very resistant to decay when put in water. For centuries, hollowed-out elm branches were used for water pipes, water-wheel paddles and boat-building. The tree has a short trunk, which divides into upward-growing branches. The leaves are up to 20cm/8in long. The dark red flowers appear in late winter before the leaves.

The seeds are carried in papery discs known as samaras.

The leaves have coarse, double teeth and have unequal sides where they join the stalk.

## IDENTIFICATION

- The bark is grey-brown, with cracks.
- The buds are red-brown.
- The leaves are dull green and rough above, lighter and heavily furred below.
- The flowers are purplish-red in clusters.
- The fruits are flat, papery, hairy discs.

## English Elm

*Ulmus procera*

The English elm is native to England, but it also grows throughout central and southern Europe. It is a stately tree, growing up to 35m/115ft tall, with long, twisted branches. The bark is dark brown with deep cracks. The dark green leaves, which are up to 10cm/4in long, are similar to those of the wych elm, and turn golden-yellow in autumn. The dark red flowers develop into samaras. English elms were almost wiped out by Dutch elm disease.

## FACT FILE

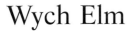

**Region of origin** Europe from Spain to Russia including western Scandinavia.

**Height** 30m/100ft

**Shape** Broadly spreading

**Deciduous**

**Pollinated** Wind

**Leaf shape** Oval to obovate

# Common Alder

*Alnus glutinosa*

This tree has always been associated with water. It thrives in damp, waterlogged conditions close to rivers and marshy ground, where it creates its own oxygen supply. Alder timber is waterproof and has been used to make products as diverse as boats and water pipes. It also forms the foundations of many of the buildings in Venice. The leaves emerge from the bud orange-brown in colour, then turn a very dark green. The male and female catkins are borne on the same tree; the females develop into small brown cones.

▲ *The cones remain on the tree until the next spring.*

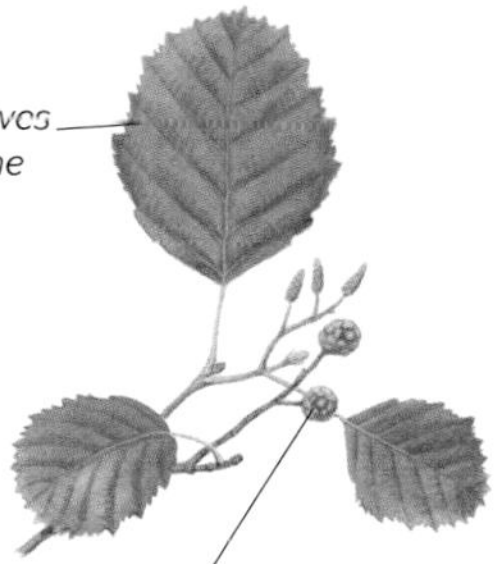

*The leaves have fine teeth.*

*The young cones are green before ripening to brown.*

## IDENTIFICATION

- The bark is dark grey-brown.
- The buds are greenish-purple.
- The leaves are up to 10cm/4in long, oval, with fine teeth, shiny dark green above and pale grey-green beneath.
- The flowers are catkins: the females red and upright; the males greenish-yellow and drooping.
- The fruits are small brown cones, which begin to grow in summer.

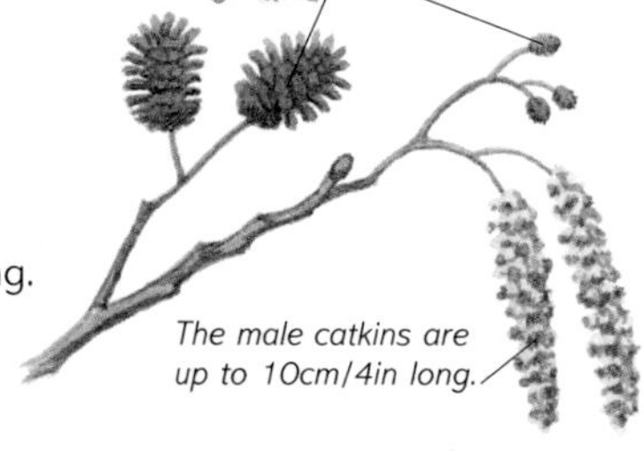

*The young, reddish, female catkins (right) ripen into small brown cones (left).*

*The male catkins are up to 10cm/4in long.*

FACT FILE

**Region of origin**
Whole of Europe into western Asia and south to North Africa.
**Height** 25m/80ft
**Shape** Broadly conical
**Deciduous**
**Pollinated** Wind
**Leaf shape** Obovate

# European Lime

Common lime *Tilia* x *europaea*

This is a hybrid between the small-leaved and large-leaved limes, and occurs naturally throughout Europe wherever the ranges of the parents overlap. Although not as elegant as its parents, and rather often attacked by aphids in summer, it is regularly planted in towns and cities for shade and ornament.

## IDENTIFICATION

- The bark is grey to grey-brown.
- The buds are ovoid and reddish-brown.
- The leaves are dull green above and paler beneath.
- The flowers are yellow, fragrant and borne in drooping clusters that hang from yellowish-green bracts.
- The fruit is ovoid, ribbed and hairy.

New leaves ▶ emerge from the buds.

The clusters of flowers hang down from a bract.

## FACT FILE

**Region of origin** Most of Europe.
**Height** 40m/130ft
**Shape** Broadly columnar
**Deciduous**
**Pollinated** Insect
**Leaf shape** Broadly ovate

# Small-leaved Lime

*Tilia cordata*

This tree grows naturally in most of Europe from Portugal to the Caucasus Mountains. It is tall (up to 30m/100ft), column-like and long-lived: some trees are believed to be over 2,000 years old. The bark is grey and smooth on young trees, becoming darker, with large cracks or flakes. The leaves are heart-shaped, glossy dark green above, paler beneath. The flowers are white and carried in clusters hanging from bracts. The fruits (shown here) are small, greenish-white and faintly ribbed.

# Large-leaved Lime

*Tilia platyphyllos*

Large-leaved lime is a ▶ large tree with huge saucer-size leaves.

This splendid, large, domed-top tree has a clean, straight trunk and graceful arching branches. Unlike the European lime, it does not suffer from aphid attack in the summer, so anything that stays for long under its branches will not be coated with the aphids' sticky excrement. Like all lime flowers, the clusters hang from a bract, which in this case is greenish-white.

The rounded leaves have sharp teeth and a pointed tip.

## IDENTIFICATION

- The bark is light grey.
- The buds are long, dark red and ovoid.
- The leaves are up to 15cm/6in across, deep green above and light green below.
- The flowers are pale yellow and fragrant.
- The fruit is pale green and pea-shaped.

The tree has a more rounded shape than the European lime.

### FACT FILE

**Region of origin** Europe into south-western Asia.
**Height** 30m/100ft
**Shape** Broadly columnar
**Deciduous**
**Pollinated** Insect
**Leaf shape** Broadly ovate

# Silver Lime

*Tilia tomentosa*

This handsome pyramid-shaped tree, which grows up to 30m/100ft tall, is native to the Balkans, Hungary, Russia and into western Asia. It has upright branches with striking two-coloured leaves, which are dark green and crinkled above and covered with silvery-white hair beneath. The bark is greenish-grey and slightly ribbed. The flowers are dull white and hang in clusters of 5–10 from yellowish-green bracts. The fruit is green, ovoid and covered with little warts.

# Narrow-leaved Ash

*Fraxinus angustifolia*

This elegant tree has, as its name suggests, the narrowest leaves of any ash. These give the tree an open, feathery look. It is a fast-growing tree that was first introduced into north-western Europe in 1800. Its flowers appear on bare twigs in late spring, and the seeds are enclosed in thin, papery fruits. These are borne in hanging fawn clusters known as "keys", which stay on the tree well into winter. There are several different types of *Fraxinus angustifolia*, including 'Raywood', which has leaves that turn plum-purple in autumn.

▲ *This graceful tree has well-spaced branches and light, airy leaves.*

*The glossy green leaflets are up to 10cm/4in long.*

## IDENTIFICATION

- The bark is grey-brown with narrow but deep vertical cracks.

- The buds are dark brown.

- The leaves are pinnate, with up to 13 lance-like, sharply toothed, glossy dark green leaflets.

- The flowers are tiny, green or purple.

- The fruits are flattened, winged seeds, up to 4cm/1½in long.

## FACT FILE

**Region of origin**
Southern Europe, North Africa and western Asia.
**Height** 25m/80ft
**Shape** Broadly columnar
**Deciduous**
**Pollinated** Insect
**Leaf shape** Pinnate

# Common Ash

*Fraxinus excelsior*

The ash "keys" are borne in clusters.

The common ash is one of the largest of all European deciduous trees and is found growing wild from the Pyrenees to the Caucasus Mountains. It has a long, straight trunk with little branching. One easy way to recognize this tree is by its velvet-black winter buds. An unusual feature of common ash trees is that, while most have either male or female flowers, some have both and some have flowers that are both male and female. Ash produces strong, white timber that is used to make items that need to be strong and impact-resistant, such as oars and hockey sticks.

Each leaflet is up to 12cm/4½in long.

The buds are black and surrounded here by purple flowers.

## IDENTIFICATION

- The bark is pale fawn, becoming grey and cracked.

- The buds are velvet-black and cone-shaped.

- The leaves are pinnate, with up to 12 pairs of shallow, toothed leaflets, dark green above and pale green beneath.

- The flowers are a mixture of purple, green and yellow and produced in great quantities in spring.

Male and female flowers are sometimes on the same tree.

## FACT FILE

**Region of origin** Europe.
**Height** 40m/130ft
**Shape** Broadly columnar
**Deciduous**
**Pollinated** Insect
**Leaf shape** Pinnate

# Hornbeam

*Carpinus betulus*

The fruits are ribbed nuts held in a three-lobed bracts, which are borne in pairs on hanging spikes.

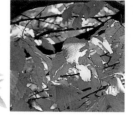

The hornbeam is sometimes confused with a beech tree because of its silver-grey bark and similar leaf. However, hornbeam bark is far more angular than beech bark, and the leaves have teeth. The timber is solid and hard and has a white, crisp look. It was traditionally used for making butchers' chopping blocks.

## IDENTIFICATION

- The bark is silvery-grey.
- The buds are pale brown.
- The leaves are oval, up to 10cm/4in long, dark green above and paler beneath.
- The flowers are catkins: greenish-yellow (male) and green with crimson styles (female).
- The fruit is a small nut contained in a bract.

### FACT FILE

**Region of origin**
Central Europe, including southern Britain to south-western Asia.
**Height** 30m/100ft
**Shape** Broadly spreading
**Deciduous**
**Pollinated** Wind
**Leaf shape** Ovate

---

# Hop Hornbeam

*Ostrya carpinifolia*

The leaves have double teeth and sharp points.

This distinctive ornamental tree is mainly known for its hop-like fruits, which, when ripe, hang in clusters of buff-coloured, overlapping, papery scales, enclosing a small brown nut. Mature trees have long, low, horizontal branches.

The hop-like fruits grow in clusters of up to 15.

## IDENTIFICATION

- The bark is smooth and brown-grey, later flaking.
- Buds are green and thin.
- The leaves are up to 10cm/4in long, dark green above and paler beneath.
- The flowers are catkins: the males are yellow and drooping, the females small and green.
- The fruit is papery and holds a single nut.

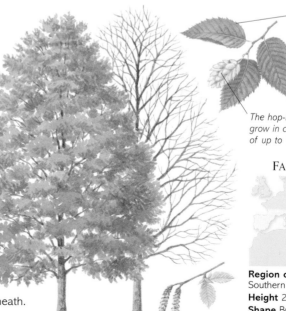

Male catkins are up to 10cm/4in long.

### FACT FILE

**Region of origin**
Southern Europe to Iran.
**Height** 20m/65ft
**Shape** Broadly spreading
**Deciduous**
**Pollinated** Wind
**Leaf shape** Ovate

# English Oak

Common oak *Quercus robur*

This is one of the most familiar trees in forests, woods, parks and gardens across Europe. It is long-lived, with many specimens over 1,000 years old; three are thought to be 1,500 years old. It is best known for its brown acorns, which usually grow in pairs and fall to the ground in autumn.

The leaves have either no stalk or a very short one.

The male catkins appear in spring.

One-third of the acorn is in a shallow cup.

### IDENTIFICATION

- The bark is pale grey and smooth, later cracked.
- The buds are light brown.
- The leaves are up to 10cm/4in long, dull dark green, with 3–6 pairs of rounded lobes.
- The male flowers are green catkins; the females tiny greenish-white flowers.
- The fruit is a dark brown acorn in a cup.

The trunk becomes twisted with age.

FACT FILE

**Region of origin** All of Europe from Ireland to the Caucasus and north to Scandinavia.
**Height** 35m/115ft
**Shape** Broadly spreading
**Deciduous**
**Pollinated** Wind
**Leaf shape** Elliptic to obovate

# Turkey Oak

*Quercus cerris*

This tall tree is the fastest-growing of all the oaks. It has been planted across Europe for centuries. The leaves differ from those of the English oak in having 7–14 lobes, which are more triangular than rounded.

The acorn cups are covered in whiskers.

FACT FILE

### IDENTIFICATION

- The bark is dark grey.
- The buds are pale brown.
- The leaves are up to 12cm/5in long, dull green, becoming shiny, above and paler below.
- The male flowers are yellow catkins; the females ovoid with yellowish scales.
- The fruit is a narrow acorn in a hairy cup.

The trunk is straight and the bark is deeply cracked.

**Region of origin** Central and southern Europe.
**Height** 35m/115ft
**Shape** Broadly spreading
**Deciduous**
**Pollinated** Wind
**Leaf shape** Elliptic to obovate

# Sweet Chestnut

Spanish chestnut *Castanea sativa*

This fast-growing tree is native to the Mediterranean but has been widely cultivated elsewhere in Europe. Romans used the chestnuts as food for themselves and their animals; they are still widely eaten, but must be cooked. The sharply toothed leaves turn golden-brown in autumn.

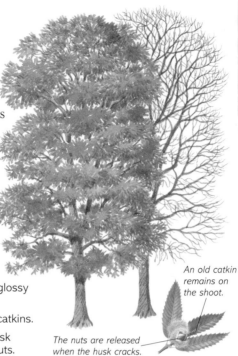

▲ *The chestnut.*

## IDENTIFICATION

- The bark is smooth and grey, later developing spiral cracks.
- The buds are round and reddish-brown.
- The leaves are up to 20cm/8in long, glossy dark green with a sharply pointed tip.
- The flowers grow together on yellow catkins.
- The fruit is a spiny greenish-yellow husk containing up to three edible brown nuts.

*The nuts are released when the husk cracks.*

*An old catkin remains on the shoot.*

### FACT FILE

**Region of origin**
Southern Europe, North Africa, south-western Asia.
**Height** 30m/100ft
**Shape** Broadly columnar
**Deciduous**
**Pollinated** Insect
**Leaf shape** Oblong

# Yellow Buckeye

Sweet buckeye *Aesculus flava*

This handsome, round-topped tree was introduced into Europe as early as 1764. *Flava* means yellow and refers to the yellow flowers that appear in early summer. This is one of the best horse chestnuts for autumn colour: the leaves turn a stunning orange-red in early autumn.

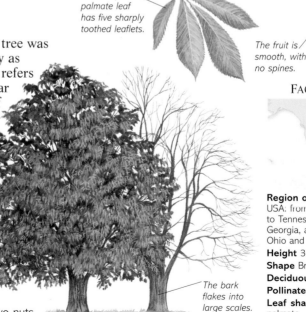

*The compound palmate leaf has five sharply toothed leaflets.*

*The fruit is smooth, with no spines.*

### FACT FILE

**Region of origin**
USA: from Pennsylvania to Tennessee and Georgia, and west into Ohio and Illinois.
**Height** 30m/100ft
**Shape** Broadly conical
**Deciduous**
**Pollinated** Insect
**Leaf shape** Compound palmate

## IDENTIFICATION

- The bark is brown-grey.
- The leaves are up to 15cm/6in long and dark green.
- The flowers are yellow with a pink blotch and borne in upright clusters.
- The fruit is a smooth husk with two nuts.

*The bark flakes into large scales.*

# Common Horse Chestnut

*Aesculus hippocastanum*

The horse chestnut is one of the most impressive of all broadleaf trees. It is tall and spreading, with a sturdy trunk and large domed top, and has interesting features to spot throughout the year. In early spring, it has large, reddish-brown winter buds covered in a sticky resin; in late spring, it is covered with its "candles" of creamy-white flowers; and in autumn, its leaves turn gold and red and the "conkers" ripen and fall to the ground.

The flowers are borne in upright clusters.

► Chestnut leaves.

## IDENTIFICATION

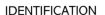

- The bark is orange-brown to grey.

- The buds are red-brown and sticky.

- The leaves are up to 30cm/12in long, dark green, with 5–7 leaflets.

- The flowers are creamy-white with yellow or pink blotches.

- The fruit is a husk containing one rounded nut ("conker") or 2–3 flattened ones.

The spiny husks crack open to reveal a "conker" inside.

### FACT FILE

**Region of origin**
Albania and Greece.
**Height** 30m/100ft
**Shape** Broadly columnar
**Deciduous**
**Pollinated** Insect
**Leaf shape** Compound palmate

The leaf buds are covered by dark scales.

# Red Horse Chestnut

*Aesculus* x *carnea*

This popular tree is a hybrid beween *Aesculus hippocastanum* (the common horse chestnut) and *Aesculus pavia* (a North American species). It is thought to have originated in Germany in the early 1800s. It is a round-headed, spreading tree, similar to the common horse chestnut but smaller in all its parts. It seldom grows taller than 20m/65ft. Its leaflets are dark green and crinkled, with broad teeth, and its flowers, which are deep pink to red, are borne in upright clusters in late spring. The conkers are similar to the common horse chestnut's, but usually have no spines.

# Ash-leaved Maple

Box elder *Acer negundo*

This small to medium-sized maple is found growing wild across North America, particularly alongside rivers and in moist soils. The name "box" comes from the fact that the timber is white and dense, like boxwood. The leaves do not look like the one on the Canadian flag, which is the classic maple leaf, because they are pinnate, with up to seven leaflets. The male flowers are tassel-like with long, drooping stamens, while the females soon develop the familiar seed wings. The ash-leaved maple is widely planted in European towns, parks and gardens for ornament and shade.

The winged seeds hang in clusters.

The leaves are a different shape to those of most maples.

## IDENTIFICATION

■ The bark is brown to silvery-grey, thin and smooth.

■ The buds are small, silvery-white and silky.

■ The leaves are pinnate, with each leaflet about 10cm/4in long and sometimes lobed. They are rich green above, lighter beneath.

■ Both male and female flowers are borne on separate trees in spring as the leaves emerge.

■ The fruits are pairs of winged seeds, ripening from green to brown.

FACT FILE

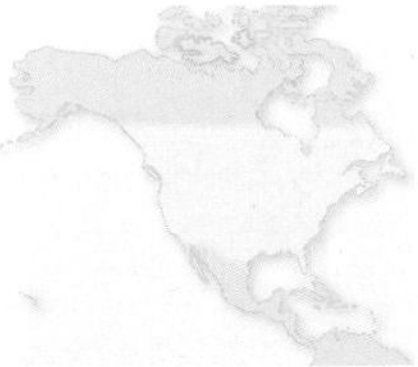

**Region of origin**
North America.
**Height** 20m/65ft
**Shape** Broadly columnar
**Deciduous**
**Pollinated** Insect
**Leaf shape** Pinnate

# Sycamore

*Acer pseudoplatanus*

The sycamore is one of the most common northern temperate trees. It grows wild in many parts of Europe, and has been planted in Britain. It is hardy, very fast-growing, and resistant to strong, salt-laden winds. It is also able to tolerate atmospheric pollution, and so is popular in towns and cities. The bark flakes attractively to reveal pinkish-orange patches below. The new leaves turn from bronze-yellow to deep green within two weeks of emerging from the bud. The winged seeds are grouped in clusters from early summer.

*The flowers are borne in narrow clusters of up to 100.*

## IDENTIFICATION

- The bark is grey and smooth, becoming greyish-pink and flaking.

- The buds are ovoid and green.

- The leaves are up to 20cm/8in across, a dull deep green above, pale bluish-green beneath, and have five lobes with big teeth.

- The flowers are small, yellowish-green and borne in hanging clusters as the leaves emerge.

- The fruits are pairs of winged seeds, each wing measuring 2.5cm/1in long.

*The winged seeds are red-green, ripening to brown in mid-autumn.*

## FACT FILE

**Region of origin**
Europe from the Pyrenees in Spain to the Carpathians in the Ukraine.
**Height** 30m/100ft
**Shape** Broadly columnar
**Deciduous**
**Pollinated** Insect
**Leaf shape** Palmate

# GLOSSARY

**Axil** Upper angle between leaf stalk and leaf.

**Bipinnate** *(of leaves)* A leaf composed of a stalk bearing two rows of smaller stalks, each of which has pairs of leaflets on either side of it, such as the mimosa.

**Bract** A modified leaf or scale placed below the calyx.

**Calyx** Collective name for sepals, at base of flower below petals; these protect the developing flower bud.

**Cambium** A layer of cells under the bark, from which annual growth of bark and wood occurs.

**Catkin** A cylindrical cluster of male or female flowers.

**Chlorophyll** Green colouring matter of plants.

**Chloroplast** Part of tree cell containing chlorophyll.

**Compound** *(of leaves)* A leaf divided into leaflets.

**Compound palmate** *(of leaves)* A leaf divided into three or more leaflets all starting at the same point on the stalk, such as the horse chestnut.

**Cone** A woody structure, often conical, bearing seeds on its scales.

**Cordate** *(of leaves)* Heart-shape, such as the katsura tree.

**Cuticle** Protective film on leaves.

**Deciduous** Shedding leaves annually or seasonally.

**Drupe** Fleshy fruit containing one seed with hard cover, for example plum.

**Elliptic** *(of leaves)* Oval in shape, with widest point at mid-section, such as the bay laurel.

**Epidermis** Protective outer layer of cells on leaves and stalks.

**Evergreen** Bearing leaves all year.

**Fastigiate** *(of trees)* Having a conical or tapering outline.

**Heartwood** Solid wood within inner core of tree trunk.

**Hybrid** A tree with "parents" from different species.

**Lanceolate** *(of leaves)* Narrow oval shape, tapering to point, such as the Tibetan cherry.

**Lenticel** A breathing hole in bark.

**Linear** *(of leaves)* Narrow, elongated, such as the yew.

**Lobed** *(of leaves)* Having rounded indentations, such as the oak.

**Meristem** Growing tissue in trees.

**Midrib** Main vein of a leaf, running down its centre.

**Needle** A slender, elongated leaf.

**Oblong** *(of leaves)* Being longer than broad, with parallel sides, such as the sweet chestnut.

**Obovate** *(of leaves)* Egg-shaped, with broadest end farthest from stem, such as the hawthorn.

**Orbicular** *(of leaves)* Round, such as the hazel.

**Osmosis** Transfer of solutions between porous partitions; process whereby liquid moves from one cell to another.

**Ovate** *(of leaves)* Egg-shaped, with broadest end nearest stem, such as the box.

**Ovoid** *(of flowers or fruit)* Egg-shaped.

**Ovule** Female reproductive structure, which develops into a seed after fertilization.

**Palmate** *(of leaves)* Hand- or palm-like, such as the sycamore.

**Phloem** Soft tissue within the tree trunk.

**Photosynthesis** Use of sunlight to create nutrients within leaves.

**Pinnate** *(of leaves)* Having leaflets in pairs on either side of the leaf stalk, such as the ash.

**Samara** A winged fruit, for example, ash "key".

**Sapwood** Soft wood between heartwood and bark.

**Scale** A small, modified leaf, such as the cypress.

**Sepal** Protector of developing flower bud, grouped as a calyx.

**Simple** *(of leaves)* Not divided into leaflets.

**Stamen** Male part of a flower; releases pollen.

**Stigma** Tip of female reproductive organ in a flower; receives pollen.

**Stomata** Tiny breathing holes in the epidermis of leaves.

**Transpiration** Loss of moisture through evaporation.

**Trifoliate** *(of leaves)* Having three leaflets.

**Xylem** Woody tissue within the tree trunk.

# INDEX